Murder Takes a Swing

Book 9

A Dodo Dorchester
Mystery

By

Ann Sutton

High stakes, dark secrets, murder and mayhem. Can Dodo find the killer of Rupert's polo teammate without endangering their love in the process?

In Murder Takes A Swing, Dodo Dorchester finds herself drawn deep into the glamorous world of polo when one of her beaus' teammates is found murdered the night after their victorious first game of the season.

With the sport of kings as its backdrop, this gripping and unputdownable page-turner will keep you on the edge of your seat as Rupert's friends and teammates become the prime suspects in this deadly game of hidden secrets.

Dodo must use her wits to untangle a web of deceit and betrayal that threatens to unravel everything Rupert thought he knew about his friends. Will she be able to solve the case before the killer strikes again? Can their developing relationship endure the strain?

Full of charm, and suspense, this delightful 1920s cozy mystery will transport you back in time to a world of adventure, and danger, keeping you on the edge of your seat until the very last twist.

Perfect for fans of classic murder mystery novels and historical whodunnits, this is a book you won't want to miss. So, grab your mallet and join the game – the stakes are high and the secrets are deadly.

Published by

Wild Poppy Publishing LLC
Highland, UT 84003

Distributed by Wild Poppy Publishing

Cover design by Julie Matern
Cover Design ©2023 Wild Poppy Publishing LLC

Edited by Jolene Perry

Dedicated to Gabriel Matern

Style Note

I am a naturalized American citizen born and raised in the United Kingdom. I have readers in America, the UK, Australia, Canada and beyond. But my book is set in the United Kingdom.

So which version of English should I choose?

I chose American English as it is my biggest audience, my family learns this English and my editor suggested it was the most logical.

This leads to criticism from those in other English-speaking countries, but I have neither the time nor the resources to do a special edition for each country.

I do use British words, phrases and idioms whenever I can (unless my editor does not understand them and then it behooves me to change it so that it is not confusing to my readers).

Titles and courtesy titles of the British nobility are complicated and somewhat dynamic through the ages. Earls, dukes and marquises have titles that are different from their family names. After extensive study on honorary titles and manners of address I have concluded that to the average reader it is all rather confusing and complicated. Earls, dukes and marquises have titles that are different from their family names which would be hard for readers to follow.

Therefore, in an attempt to eliminate this confusion, I have made the editorial decision to call Dodo's father Lord Dorchester rather than Lord Trent and her mother Lady Guinevere rather than Lady Trent.

Table of Contents

Murder Takes a Swing

List of characters

Lizzie Perkins	Dodo's maid
Ernest Scott	Lizzie's beau
Guinevere Dorchester	Dodo's mother
Alfred Dorchester	Dodo's father
Didi Dorchester	Dodo's sister

Polo Team

Rupert Danforth	Dodo's beau
Jasper Boynton	
Raphael (Rafe) Alleyn	
Hugh Cavendish	

Others

Juliette Honeybourne	Jasper's girlfriend

Rosamund Ainsworth	Hugh's girlfriend
Poppy Drinkwater	Juliette's friend
Florence Tingey	Rafe Alleyn's ex
Max Fortnon	Opposing team member

Chapter 1

S lathered in sweat, the two majestic steeds on an inevitable crash course, Dodo Dorchester covered her eyes, unable to bear the impending collision. When a loud roar from the boisterous crowd indicated a near miss, she risked a peek. The two snorting animals, tossing their heads, parted company unhurt. However, the white polo ball remained in the same spot on the grass. Both riders had apparently missed.

Crack!

Another rider's mallet successfully struck the wooden sphere sending it out of the crush of pounding horses and men, toward the opposing team's goal. Pulse pounding in her ears, Dodo watched with bated breath, clapping gloved hands as Rupert Danforth swung his horse in the direction of the ball, grass sods flying behind his impressive mount as he picked up speed. His white jersey billowed in the breeze, blue eyes fixed on the goal ahead, single minded, mallet raised.

Thwack!

The small ball flew just above the top of the redolent grass blades, directly toward the target, as Dodo clasped her hands, heart in her throat.

Goal!

The boisterous crowd went wild.

Dodo choked on a surge of pride as Rupert stood upright in his stirrups, arms raised in triumph as the umpire signaled the end of the second chukka. The seven minutes had flown by.

She had insisted on coming to the polo game alone, anxious about Rupert's safety, worried that her ignorance of the game would make her appear a fool if she were with company. But now, she had no one to celebrate with. She glanced to her left and right as other spectators gobbled to each other like oversized turkeys, having to be content with her own thrill at Rupert's superior skill.

He had claimed to be a middling, average player but from what she had observed thus far, he had woefully downplayed his abilities.

1

His position was that of the coveted third player, and he had scored both of the team's goals. The opposing team had scored only once.

The helmeted players all trotted off the field, their horses whinnying and bickering like old ladies at a church coffee morning. The riders would change to fresh horses for the next chukka after a fifteen-minute rest for halftime. Though impulse directed her to run over and congratulate Rupert, she understood that such things were frowned upon in the sport. Any congratulations would have to wait until the game was completely over.

This was the opening game of the season, and the weak April sunshine did little to warm her, but she was grateful it had not rained—yet. She pulled up the collar of her light gray cashmere coat as the other spectators rushed onto the field to 'tread-in' the divots made by the horses. Having been warned of this practice by Rupert, she had reluctantly donned some ugly, green rubber boots and tentatively walked out onto the muddy field.

Watching the other observers dig in their boots, she mimicked their actions, kicking her heel into the muddy grass to smash the upended turf back into the ground. It was rather fun. She searched ahead to find another hole and repeated the action breathing in the earthy smell. She had fixed six such holes before the umpire indicated that it was time to return to the spectator's area. Turning, she bumped into another guest.

"I'm terribly sorry—" she began, as her eyes met those of the one and only Veronica Shufflebottom.

Veronica's cat-like pupils widened under her platinum waves. "As I live and breathe—Dodo Dorchester."

Dodo was fashioning a suitable zinger in her head when the umpire rushed over. "Ladies, I must insist that you hurry. The next chukka is about to begin."

Veronica followed on Dodo's hideous, rubber heels, her own impractical heels sinking into the sod. Instead of finding her friends, Veronica stood right next to Dodo.

"Aren't you with a group?" Dodo asked irritably, desperately hoping she could offload the annoying woman from her schooldays.

"Of course, but I'm late. I arrived as everyone rushed onto the field." Veronica's voice was like an untuned violin. "I didn't have a moment to find them." Along with the unwise choice of footwear, the aggravating woman was wearing an outrageously large hat as if she thought she was attending Ascot. Veronica lifted her head to check the crowds. "And you?"

Had Veronica heard that Dodo and Rupert Danforth were now an item? The last time Dodo had seen Veronica was after solving a murder at her cousin's estate on Dartmoor. At that time, Veronica was being carted off to a private clinic by the compassionate Rupert, to overcome an opium addiction.

"Uh, no, actually. I'm here alone. I'm meeting up with some people after the game."

Veronica frowned, incredulous. "Alone?"

"Well, I'm here to watch one of the players." Dodo had no desire to explain anything to the girl who had bullied her mercilessly at school.

Veronica's sharp eyes narrowed. "A player?" She examined Dodo's face, then clapped her hands together. "You and Rupert! I should have guessed." She let out a throaty giggle. "You are *perfect* for each other."

Now it was time for Dodo to narrow *her* eyes and search her nemesis's face for signs of jealousy.

Veronica flicked a manicured hand. "You're welcome to him, darling! He's too much of a goody-two shoes for my taste." She became serious for a moment. "Though I do owe him for helping me out last year."

The eight players trotted out on fresh horses and Veronica's unwelcome presence stuck to Dodo like a parasitic barnacle.

"Ooh! There's Oliver Andrews!" Veronica's high-pitched screech was reminiscent of brakes squealing to a stop. Several heads turned in her direction wearing large frowns. "Bye-bye, toots!" she cried. She blew Dodo a kiss, weaving in the direction of her friend and hitting people on the head with her outsized brim. Dodo was more than a little relieved.

The ground umpire rolled out the starting ball and the players took off again. The field was larger than Dodo had expected and when the ball was on the other side, she could not see Rupert's face. It had also taken a while to remember that once a goal was scored, the whole game reversed so that the team's new aim was to get the ball through the goal at the opposite end. She had asked Rupert to give her a crash course before coming but until she saw the players in action, it hadn't made much sense.

A shout went up from another part of the crowd and a judge raised a flag as a player on the opposing team raised his arms. The score was now two to two. All the players thundered toward the other end of the field, but Rupert managed to interrupt the ball's flow and knock it back toward their new goal. Dodo watched in wonder as the beautiful beasts turned sharply, speeding to pursue the ball in a new direction, more grass clods flying in their wake. It was all so different from the skills required from the racehorses her father owned.

Captivated by the action, she was surprised when the whistle blew for the end of the third seven-minute chukka. Her eyes trained on Rupert's horse, she watched as the players cantered back to the stables for the third time. Before meeting Rupert, she had no idea that each chukka required a new horse. No wonder it was called the sport of kings.

Rather than bump into Veronica again, Dodo stayed on the sidelines as other spectators rushed to dig in the divots. A cloud passed over the sun, plunging the field into shadow and causing the temperature to drop. She looked up to check for the chance of rain but thankfully, the cloud was not dark. She would be ready for the tea tent when the game finished. At the thought, she experienced a little kick of anticipation. That was when Rupert was going to introduce her to the rest of the team.

The players filed out for the final chukka, their horses neighing with pleasure, their hands busy with whips and mallets. Dodo's spirits rose as Rupert swung at the ball setting it flying. All eight players ran their horses forward, the mounted umpires keeping to the edges of play.

4

A player from the other team intercepted the ball and sent it sailing toward the goal at the opposite end of the field. Pulling on the reins, the players changed direction yet again. Tails and manes braided, the magnificent animals bolted forward, muscles rippling through their shiny coats.

Another player on Rupert's team swung and connected with the ball sending it back the way it had come, right into Rupert's path. He turned his horse and lifted the mallet to swing, the loud *crack* of precision rippling through the air. Dodo's heart began to race along with the horses. Would Rupert's ball make it through the goal posts before the end of the game?

Squinting to see the ball, Dodo saw that it stopped several yards in front of the goal as Rupert and a rival player scrambled to reach it first. Rupert 'bumped' the other player's horse with his and Dodo winced, but other than moving the opposing horse out of the way, neither steed appeared injured.

Just as Rupert raised his mallet again another stocky rider 'bumped' Rupert's horse, and hooked his mallet, disengaging the instrument from Rupert's hand. The crowd groaned.

"Mallet!" shouted Rupert, as another team member ran his horse in front of the pair, whacking the ball successfully through the goal posts. The spectators erupted, and Dodo did a little jig as the final whistle split the air.

After hurrying to her car to change out of the hideous boots and into proper shoes, Dodo made her way to the relative warmth of the tea tent where she had arranged to meet Rupert after the game. The pavilion was quite large with countless round tables scattered about. Long trestle tables at the back held silver urns and platters boasting a variety of tea cakes. She grabbed a hot cup of tea and found a corner to hide from Veronica. From there she was able to watch the cold crowd entering.

Though most of the spectators were men, there was a smattering of women here to support friends and family members. Other than the offensive Veronica, Dodo did not recognize anyone. This was a circle in which her family did not run.

Most of the women wore dark coats and hats to match the necessary wellies and Dodo made a mental note to blend in better next time—a thing it was counter to her nature to do.

A fracas caused Dodo to turn her attention back to the tea table. *Veronica.* Dressed in that fuchsia coat more suitable for a jazz club than a game of polo, she was haranguing the poor maid at the tea service about not giving her enough sugar. Did Veronica have to make every event a drama?

Dodo's gaze wandered back to the tent entrance. A rather stiff looking, middle-aged woman was encouraging a pretty, blonde in her early twenties, to fetch her some tea. They had to be mother and daughter since they shared a nose and a strong brow, though the girl's delicate eyes must have come from her father. The graceful young woman nodded and began to make her way through the crowd while her mother secured a central table.

Another older woman with steel gray hair and a sharply hooked nose, glared around the busy space, her sharp eyes finally settling on the woman with the daughter. She stomped her way over to their table, elbowing people as she waded through. Clinging to the fashions of another era, she finally slumped into a chair and began hitting the table with her fist. Too far away, Dodo could not hear the words that spilled from her slack mouth.

Next, a crowd of rowdy young men slouched their way to the cake table and behind them Dodo spotted a handsome fellow, about Rupert's age, in full military uniform. He wore a tightly clipped mustache and held his cap under his arm. Scanning the room, his eyes did not light up with recognition. Instead, he strode to the tea table, then stood, nursing the cup and saucer, watching everyone in the room.

A buxom girl about her own age, bounced past the soldier, though he only gave her a cursory glance, which was strange since she was striking both in figure and clothing. Dressed in red from head to foot, including her Wellingtons, she walked with purpose toward the tea table. As she ordered some refreshment, the lively animation of her features only enhanced her attractions. Tea in hand, she meandered through the tables, her rich brown hair peeking out from under a classy hat with a stylish feather that Dodo would have been happy to wear herself.

When the girl in red arrived at the table with the ethereal girl and her mother, a huge smile split the brunette's face and she finally caught the appreciation of the standing soldier.

Dodo's attention was caught by a movement near the entrance. *Rupert!* Her emotions ran over like a newly opened bottle of champagne. He was waving, back in regular clothes, grinning like a schoolboy. His delightful, slightly chipped front tooth on full display for all to see.

"What did you think?" he asked, his face begging for her approval as he slid into the chair next to her, sliding an arm around her shoulders.

"I was absolutely riveted the whole time," she admitted. "How have I never caught the bug before?"

He oozed with satisfaction at her response and she was relieved that she didn't have to pretend; she had thoroughly enjoyed the sport. Which was convenient as polo was clearly very important to him. He grabbed her hand and kissed the knuckles, his hot breath hovering over her skin.

"You don't know how glad I am to hear it!" Still holding her hand, he stood. "Now, let me introduce you to everyone."

Holding her tea in one hand, her other loosely held in his, Dodo let Rupert guide her over to the very table she had been watching. They had since been joined by three of the other players and the military man, to make quite a crowd. Rupert pulled over two folding chairs.

"Everyone! This is Lady Dorothea Dorchester. My sweetheart."

Her heart danced a jig at the term of endearment as she said, "Oh, please! Call me Dodo."

"Dorchester?" asked the hooked-nosed lady, holding a pince-nez to her eyes and squinting up at Dodo. "Any relation to the Dowager Countess Dorchester?"

"Why, yes!" exclaimed Dodo. "She is my grandmother."

Nodding, the lady explained, "We met in the late years of the last century at some pheasant shoots in Scotland." Dodo wondered how her progressive grandmother had liked the formal woman before her.

"It is a pleasure to meet you," she said holding out her hand then sitting on the edge of the seat Rupert had brought over.

"Juliette Honeybourne," announced the lovely girl, now sitting exceptionally close to one of Rupert's teammates. "How do you do?" She turned to the vivacious girl in red. "And this is my good friend, Poppy Drinkwater."

Poppy flashed the bright smile Dodo had witnessed moments before. "How do you do?"

"And this rogue is, Jasper Boynton, defender extraordinaire," said Rupert, indicating her rather taciturn young man who was rocking back on his chair. Dodo nodded to them both wondering how the stern fellow had captured the heart of such a bubbly girl. "And his mother, Lady Clara Boynton," added Rupert. The acquaintance of Dodo's grandmother acknowledged her once more.

Gesturing with his hand, Rupert continued the introductions. "The hugely talented Hugh Cavendish, polo player and childhood friend, and his beloved, Lady Rosamund Ainsworth."

This pair were an obvious match, and Dodo rewarded them with a huge smile of her own.

"They will be married this summer," continued Rupert.

"Congratulations!" said Dodo, glancing to see Rupert's countenance as he said the word 'married'.

Rosamund, whom Dodo had not noticed from her corner, put down a cigarette to shake hands. Her round face framed with lush, auburn curls, she confidently held Dodo's gaze. The Viking, Hugh, wrapped a strapping arm protectively around Rosamund's broad shoulders, his grin of welcome producing an endearing dimple in one cheek.

"Very nice to finally meet the woman who has been able to tame Rupert." Hugh's booming voice fit his physique perfectly.

Dodo looked quizzically at Rupert for an explanation.

"He's kidding," Rupert assured her, shooting a side look at Hugh.

8

"I'm not," Hugh retorted, securing a colorful scarf around his neck. "You should see the long trail of woman who have tried to capture this fellow and failed. But now that I've met you, I can totally see why he is smitten."

Dodo liked Hugh immediately.

"It's true," agreed Rosamund, a small brooch peeping through the coppery curls on her shoulders.

"And finally, Raphael Alleyn. The newly single, man about town." Raphael was the slightest of the team members.

"Call me Rafe," he insisted, green, friendly eyes shining out from under soft, dark waves. "And allow me to introduce my cousin, Captain Theodore Lindley. He came to watch me play today."

The conventional captain held out a hand to Dodo, her head spinning with so many names.

She gripped it firmly. "It's a pleasure to meet you."

"We forgot to introduce Mama," said Juliette. "Mrs. Adriana Honeybourne."

Her stiff mother forced a smile that merely moved her lips, never quite reaching her eyes.

"What a jolly party we are!" sang out the sociable Poppy. "And what a thrilling game!" Dodo noticed that she tried to catch the captain's eye with her remark, but he was looking across the room.

"It was rather gripping!" agreed Juliette. "I nearly died when that chap knocked Rupert's mallet from his hand."

"Not as much as I did," added Rupert. "It's rare that I lose the grip on my mallet."

"*I* wasn't worried," declared Rafe. "I was positive I could make that goal before the whistle blew."

"I wasn't really anxious either," said Rupert. "I knew you had my back." He slapped his team mate so hard Rafe choked, and all the young people chuckled.

A howl of laughter from the other side of the tent heralded the presence of Veronica, drawing the critical eyes of Rupert's whole group.

"Veronica is here," Dodo whispered into Rupert's ear.

Rupert wrinkled his nose and whispered back, "Hopefully since we are with my friends, we can avoid her."

"Too late for me," commented Dodo. "That's why you found me skulking in the corner."

"How ghastly!" His lips brushed her ear making her stomach flip. "Did she spoil everything for you?"

"Not at all!" Dodo assured him. "Fortunately, she spotted her friends before the chukka began again."

The group of friends at the table descended into small talk, mentioning the decent spring weather and the health of the large horses, who were called ponies, much to Dodo's confusion.

About a quarter of an hour later, the two older women got to their feet.

"My driver is here to take us home," explained Lady Boynton. "But you young people will be sure to celebrate until the early hours." The sentence was delivered as a condemnation. "We shall bid you, adieu."

Once they were gone, Poppy's brows rose. "What *are* this evening's plans?"

"I booked a table at *Rive Gauche*," said Rafe with a gleam in his eye. "Does that suit everyone? Then we could go on to the *Salad Club*."

Dodo was familiar with the place. It was well respected, unlike some of the other jazz clubs around town.

"Rather!" responded Rupert.

"That's set then. Let's say we meet at the *Rive Gauche* at seven-thirty," said Rafe with a saucy wink at Poppy. "That should give you young ladies plenty of time to change."

Chapter 2

Dodo understood the power of dressing to impress more than most and used the skill to her advantage. Because of her developing relationship with Rupert, she had skipped the Paris fashion show this spring, but Renée had sent some samples and it was one of those head-turning dresses she had chosen to wear this evening.

The sensational gown was made up of two separate parts–one a simple silk sheath that hung to mid-calf and the other a complicated beaded dress that sat over the plain silk exposing it at various vantage points. The mother of pearl, silk underdress began as a flattering bandeau that sat tightly around the chest, gripping her stomach and hips, an even hem ending well above the ankle. A daringly low bodice and ultra-thin straps on the beaded over-dress, exposed the modest bandeau beneath as part of the ensemble. The encrusted gown fitted tightly across the ribs and stomach, the beads giving way to long white feathers that hung from the hips, and the uneven hem draping as low as the ankle in places. The bold, beaded head band was reminiscent of a chieftain's feather headdress with silver fabric fashioned around florists wire to resemble palm fronds that emerged from the back of the head. The perfect frame to her blunt, black bob.

The whole ensemble was quite a statement, even by Dodo's standards.

She had been vain enough to notice the appreciation of the men and the envy of the women as she and Rupert had arrived together at the upscale restaurant.

"What a simply smashing frock!" gasped Poppy.

"I agree," exclaimed Rosamund, eyes wide. "But I don't think I could pull of that look with my…generous figure."

Though Dodo and Captain Lindley had just met the group, the others were old friends and the mood around the table was casual and relaxed. Only one thing was missing to make it all perfect. Rafe. He must have been delayed.

"Can I take your order?" said a burly waiter.

Rupert glanced at his watch. "Rafe is running late as usual," he said to his teammates. "Let's get started. He'll be here soon enough."

After oysters and lobster, trout and asparagus, they were all tucking into a decadent tiramisu.

"Tell me Captain Lindley, where have you served?" asked Rupert.

He still wore his uniform but had loosened up considerably. "Please call me Theo," he began. "As a career soldier, I was fortunate enough to be posted elsewhere when the war began and thus was out of the worst of the fighting for the most part. But I have seen much of the Middle East and India."

"And what has been your favorite part of those places?" Dodo asked, her dress straining against her stomach.

"India," he said without hesitation. "It's a land of contrasts; extreme poverty versus decadent wealth. The brightest of colors amidst the dullest of fabrics. The warm summer climate, the wettest monsoon season. I enjoyed my time there very much. I hope to go back."

"It's a place I have never been, but I should like to one day," Dodo responded.

"Much as I admire the place, it can be volatile and perhaps not the safest location for tourists," he explained, wiping his tidy mustache with a crisp, white napkin. "But I look forward to a day when it is more stable."

"In that case, I shall await such a time too," she replied. "Are you between commissions at the moment, Captain?"

"I am. When Rafe invited me to watch the opening game of the season, I was more than interested. I had a go at the sport in India but was hopeless. I quite admire their skill and my cousin played very well today."

"He did," she agreed. "I wonder what has kept him this evening." She glanced at the door. "You're not staying with him, I presume."

"No. Don't want to impose. He is at an aunt's house for the game. I'm staying at my club. That way I put no one out. He must have had some business that delayed him. He'll explain it all at the club later, no doubt."

"Indeed."

"Where did you find that gown?" asked Poppy. "I simply must have one!"

Dodo explained her position as an ambassador for the House of Dubois and all that it entailed.

"So, this dress is not even for sale yet?" Poppy asked. "How simply marvelous!"

"The idea is that I wear the dress in the normal run of my life and it evokes interest. Then when it goes on sale, women are clamoring to get it."

"Brilliant! Absolutely brilliant!" Poppy took a sip from her flute. "I imagine it works like a charm."

"It does, rather," Dodo agreed.

"And you have the perfect shape for it," said Poppy without a hint of jealousy. "I may be a bit too endowed in the upstairs department, if you know what I mean." She raised her shoulders, lifting her expansive chest which would have been the envy of the whole table in a different era.

Dodo chuckled. "I'm sure the pendulum will swing back in your direction soon enough."

Though Poppy's dress was not as rich as Dodo's gown, she certainly knew how to show off her own assets to advantage. She had kept to the red pallet, but this evening the hue was a vibrant burgundy. The deep shade of crimson was the perfect complement to her dark, shiny hair and enviable complexion. Her dress plunged to a 'v', but not to excess, with a matching but deeper shape on the back, filled with strands of pearls. The straight frock fell to the floor and a simple headband with a short, deep red feather completed the sophisticated look.

"But you look lovely," Dodo assured her.

"I thought so too 'til I saw your dress!" Poppy laughed, and it was like swallows warbling. "I bought this after my fiancé and I broke things off. I suppose you might call it the revenge dress. It made me feel much better."

"Oh, I'm so sorry," responded Dodo.

"Larks! Don't be! He was a cad. Unfaithful as a Tom cat." Her delightful smile faded to a grimace. "I'm just glad I found out before the wedding." Her grip on the flute tightened. "My father died and left us with debts to pay. I have some money left to me by a grandmother, but I'm not much of a financial catch. He *said* he didn't care. Not too many men with that attitude, these days."

Dodo rested her chin in her hand. "I suppose so." Luckily, this was a problem she would never face.

"Let's change the subject, shall we?" Poppy suggested. "This is a night for fun. Possibilities."

"What about the captain?" suggested Dodo, lowering her voice. "He's a handsome man."

Poppy narrowed her eyes, glancing over at the fellow in question. "He's not bad, I suppose, but I have no desire to be married to a man in the armed forces who belongs to the whim of the government. He could be gone for years at a time. No, I need someone who will always be around."

"What about Rafe? He seems like a nice chap."

"Actually, that's why I'm here," she admitted, leaning back to put an olive between her teeth and pull it off the cocktail stick. "He's also had a recent break-up and Juliette thought we might hit it off. It's a blind date of sorts."

"And what did you think of him?" asked Dodo.

"He seems like a thoroughly nice chap, and he appeared to like me. I'm interested to see what the evening brings. I assume he got delayed and will meet us at the club."

As the waiter came to settle the bill, Dodo pushed back her chair. "If you'll excuse me, I need to go to the ladies' room."

"I shall join you," said the petite Juliette, dressed in a shimmering silver gown.

"Me too," added Rosamund, standing and shifting her peach chiffon dress over her generous hips.

The sophisticated restaurant boasted a large ladies' room with ubiquitous green marble and a smart attendant. After finishing her business, Dodo removed a lipstick tube from her clutch and began to repair her lips in front of a large, gilded mirror.

"You look fabulous," said Juliette as she washed her hands in a sink shaped like a clam shell.

"Thank you," said Dodo graciously. "You look stunning yourself. The silver is very flattering."

Juliette twisted her body to look in the mirror. "It's a terribly adventurous look for me. I'm more a floral girl really, but I must admit, I love how this makes me feel."

"That's one of the things I love about the right dress," said Dodo. "Empowerment."

Juliette gazed at her reflection.

"And I think Mr. Boynton is happy with the effect too," said Dodo with a smile. Her comment brought a hint of pink to Juliette's cheeks.

Rosamund joined them, still pulling at her dress. "I think I've put on weight since I had this made," she complained. "But I do so love my cream teas." Now that she was standing, it was apparent that the dress was a little tighter than it should have been around her middle.

"Hugh wouldn't care if you were the size of an elephant," commented Juliette. "It's obvious to anyone with eyes that he's dotty about you."

Rosamund caught their eyes in the mirror. "I know. He tells me he likes a fuller figure so there is more to hold on to." She adjusted her headpiece over the enviable auburn hair and puckered her lips. "He may just be fibbing, but it makes me feel treasured."

"He loves your soul," said Juliette running a finger over her own lips.

"Still, I'd better be careful with the scones and clotted cream or I shall burst out of my wedding dress!"

As they turned to leave, someone clattered through the door. *Veronica!*

"Oh, hello again!" her already shrill voice fueled by too much alcohol. She ran jealous eyes up and down Dodo's length. "Don't *you* look nice?"

Dodo bit her cheek.

"And who's tubby here?" said Veronica, flapping a hand toward Rosamund, whose light skin was now poppy red.

Dodo closed her eyes in horror taking a large breath. "Mind your manners, Veronica. This is Lady Rosamund Ainsworth."

"How do you do?" responded an unrepentant Veronica in a mocking tone. "What about birdie?" She tipped her head toward Juliette who was biting back a nervous smile.

"Really, Veronica! You are insulting my friends."

The attendant stood as if to come to their assistance, but Dodo held up a hand.

Veronica's left brow shot up. "Friends? I *do* beg your pardon."

"May I introduce Miss Juliette Honeybourne. Now, we must be going." Dodo turned toward the exit.

"No time for *old* friends then," spat Veronica, wobbling on her heels toward one of the lavatories.

Dodo refused to dignify the absurd comment with a response and hustled herself and the other two women out of the ladies' room.

"I really *must* apologize," Dodo remarked with embarrassment as they made their way back to the table. "Veronica Shufflebottom is *no* friend of mine I can assure you. However, I did suffer the misfortune of attending the same school and she clings to the association whenever we meet in public—which I try to avoid at all costs."

"Ah," they both uttered.

"I think we all know someone like that," said Juliette.

Rosamund was fuming.

Upon their return, everyone stood and moved to the cloakroom to retrieve their coats. As Rupert was helping Dodo slip on her winter white fur, the maître d' zigzagged through the diners, waving a paper over his head.

"Messieurs," he panted. "I have just received a phone call." He placed a hand to his chest as they all stared anxiously. "It is Monsieur Alleyn. He is dead."

Chapter 3

Rupert dropped Dodo's expensive fur to the floor and grabbed the waiter roughly by the lapel. "What did you say?"

The man's frenzied eyes enlarged, and he frowned down at Rupert's fists.

"I'm sorry," said Rupert, releasing the little man and patting his lapels. "You gave me a shock. I thought you said Rafe Alleyn, the Earl of Kent, was dead."

Taking a step back, the waiter pulled down his black jacket and straightened his tie. "I did."

Everyone began shouting at once and Rupert cried, "Quiet! Let's hear what the man has to say."

"One of the grooms from the polo club. He overheard you were going to dine here. I wrote down exactly what he said."

He proffered the paper which Rupert grabbed and read aloud. "Went back to check on a horse. Found Mr. Rafe Alleyn in a back corner..." Rupert's voice faltered "His head smashed in. Have called the police."

"My cousin is...dead?" The captain's face was pale and rigid.

Juliette began to cry. "How is it possible? We were just with him?"

"How dreadful!" exclaimed Poppy. "I shall take a taxi home. Don't worry about me."

"I'll see you to a cab," said the captain, replacing his cap.

"What can I do?" asked Jasper, any color in his complexion, gone in a flash.

Rupert turned to catch Dodo's hand. "The police have been called and Dodo has some talent in this area. We'll head over there and fill you in on what we discover."

"Are you sure?" Jasper asked, an arm around the distraught Juliette.

"Absolutely! Take Juliette home. We'll contact you as soon as we know anything. You too," he said directing his words to Hugh and Rosamund who were frozen to the spot. "They'll be getting statements from all of us soon enough."

"Could he have been trampled by a horse, do you think?" asked Rosamund, her eyes shining.

The captain came back through the door, anxiety stamped on every feature.

"That is a possibility I suppose," said Rupert. "We'll let you know what the police say."

"As his closest relative, I feel that I should accompany you," said the captain.

As gently as she could, Dodo said, "I don't think the police will take too kindly to the arrival of a crowd. We promise to keep you informed. Perhaps you can go and break the news to his mother."

As Dodo and Rupert stood on the pavement watching Rupert's friends leave, he deflated like a balloon. "Rafe is—was one of my closest friends," he said, the words getting strangled in his throat. "Part of me hopes it's a case of mistaken identity."

Dodo's heart squeezed with compassion. She placed a comforting hand on his shoulder. "What did you think when he didn't turn up to dinner?"

"You know those people who are *always* late? That was Rafe. I thought he was just being his usual self and would meet up with us at the club. I'm devastated."

The pain in his expression pierced her chest. Spying a bench, she guided Rupert to sit. "While we wait for a taxi, tell me what happened after the game."

Palm to his forehead he said, "We were high on adrenaline. Cocksure from our triumph. Rafe was singing at the top of his lungs in the stables—honestly, I'm surprised you couldn't hear him in the tea tent."

"How did the other team react to this show of bravado?"

"One of them, a player named Max, told him to pack it in, but the other players were good sports about it. It could just as easily have

18

been *their* win and they would have rubbed it in our faces too. It's all part of the culture."

"Then what happened?"

"We rewarded our ponies with apples and went back to the changing rooms. We all dressed quickly as we knew there were people waiting for us."

"Even Rafe?" she asked.

"Yes. He was eager to meet you."

"So, no joshing in the changing room?"

"No more than usual." His face crumpled with pain.

Dodo interlaced her fingers through his. They were shaking.

"What about when we all left to get ready for this evening?" she continued.

"As I told you, Rafe has an aunt near here and we are both staying there—blast! Someone will need to call her." Anxiety replaced the pain. He tapped his chin repeatedly.

Dodo ran her thumb across his cheekbone. "It can wait until we know more. She's not his mother, after all."

Rupert nodded. "I took a quick bath then hurried out to meet you. I didn't even stop to see if Rafe was back. I just assumed."

"Where does his mother live?"

"Their estate is in a little village in Essex. Rafe was an only child. Lady Alleyn will be devastated."

He dropped his head into the other hand, short breaths indicating that he was fighting back tears.

"So, Rafe did not leave the polo club at the same time as everyone else?"

"No. He said he had to run back because he'd forgotten something and would see me later."

"I wonder if he met someone or witnessed something?" she mused.

Rupert lifted tortured eyes to hers. "Yes. That might explain it."

"Are you sure you are up to going back to the polo club?" She knew that seeing the body of his friend when he was already distraught might put him over the edge.

"I have to," he moaned. "I have to see for myself, Dodo. I can't…can't believe it. Everyone loved Rafe."

But someone clearly hadn't.

"I can't have civilians trampling all over my crime scene!" The irritable voice floated from the back of the dark, pungent stables to where they stood, just outside the large barndoors. The sound of agitated horses stomping in their stalls almost drowned him out.

"I don't care *who* she knows!"

Dodo and Rupert locked eyes. Dropping Chief Inspector Blood's name had not helped. The lottery had dealt them an irascible, stubborn policeman.

The young constable, whose helmet hung too low over his eyes, and whose cheeks were flaming, came back to the entrance.

"I'm sorry, m'lady. The inspector says you can't come back."

Time to pull out the big guns. "I think Sir Matthew Cusworth will be annoyed to hear that I was denied access."

"Sir-Sir-Matthew? The-the Commissioner of Police?"

"One and the same." She narrowed her eyes.

"I'll explain the situation," the copper gasped, turning on his heels and disappearing into the dark interior once more. Only a few bare lightbulbs hung from the high ceiling.

Strains of a heated discussion made their way to the door, but she could distinguish no actual words. The sound of heavy boots crunching across the floor indicated the bobby's return.

"The inspector says he will come and speak to you in a minute."

Well, that was better than a brush off. "Certainly. Tell him to take his time," said Dodo, smoothly.

Rupert had become very quiet and just kept shaking his head. Dodo recognized the signs of shock. "Are you sure you want to stay? I completely understand if you want to go, darling. I can get a taxi back to my hotel."

Lifting his head, eyes distant, he murmured, "No. I need to know what happened. I promised the others."

Dodo squeezed his hand and wrapped her coat more tightly with the other. Her gown was wholly unsuitable for a drafty barn on a cool spring evening and given the circumstances, she felt the utter ridiculousness of the extravagant headpiece. Reaching up, she yanked off the fancy piece of millinery and held it limply at her side.

It was a clear, cloudless night and the stars were putting on a show, careless of the tragedy down below. As she waited, Dodo picked out the Big Dipper and Orion and was searching for Cassiopeia when footsteps sounded again.

Out of the darkness and into the light of the moon emerged a small, rotund man with large whiskers and a pipe between his lips. Squinting his eyes, bottom lip jutted out, he asked in a raspy voice. "Lady Dorothea?" He made no effort to shake her hand.

She switched on the aristocratic charm. "Inspector. How kind of you to give me a few minutes of your precious time."

He merely grunted, chewing on the stem of his cold pipe.

"We are close friends of the deceased. Well, my boyfriend is. Mr. Rupert Danforth. He's the captain of Lord Alleyn's polo team."

This had been the right thing to say as the inspector's eyes widened with expectation. "Ah. I've been wanting to talk to his teammates."

"You are...sure it's Rafe?" asked Rupert, the words stumbling out.

"Well, until the next of kin identify the uh, body, I cannot be one hundred per cent certain, but given that the groom recognized him, I'd say we are pretty confident."

Rupert seemed to shrink several inches.

"How was he killed?" asked Dodo, taking advantage of the inspector's improved mood.

The inspector scrunched an eye. "Beaten in the head with a polo mallet."

Rupert made a guttural sound.

"Did the killer leave any clues?" she asked.

The mask of suspicion slid back across the inspector's features.

"I should perhaps mention that I have helped Scotland Yard solve several murder cases," she stated. "Did you hear about the case of the murdered model at the British Empire Fair?"

The stummel of the inspector's pipe bounced up but not with enthusiasm.

"Of course," he growled.

"I was the inside person who helped with the investigation." She held the inspector's hostile stare.

"I don't remember seeing your name in the paper," he retorted.

She stepped closer, the sweet, earthy aroma of tobacco wafting from his coat. "That was to save my mother any anxiety, but you may contact Inspector Hornby of Scotland Yard if you doubt my claims."

The inspector's bluish nose wrinkled.

"So? Were there any clues?" she persisted.

"Not that it's any of your business, but it's hard to see back there with a lantern. The overhead lighting is weak. I shall have my men go through the straw with a fine-tooth comb at first light."

"And the weapon? Was it left at the scene or stashed with the other mallets?"

The inspector raised his considerable brows. "It was left next to the body, if you must know. But I don't hold out hope that it will hold any clues as there are plenty of gloves around this place. They'd be an idiot to use bare hands in this day and age."

Dodo addressed Rupert. "Do you bring your own mallets or are they all for general use?"

His brows knit tight, he squinted at her as if he had not understood. "What? Oh, we use several in each game especially if they get loose. I have my own, but there are always some common ones for public use."

"So, there might be lots of fingerprints on them?" she pointed out.

"Well, we wear gloves to play but the people handing them to us might not."

The inspector cleared his gravelly throat. "When did you last see Lord Alleyn?"

22

Dodo gave a detailed report of the group meeting at the tea tent and the plans to meet up at the restaurant and then go on to a dance club. "But Rupert just told me that Rafe returned to the stable area and told him he would meet us all later."

A dark car pulled up behind them and a gray-haired man holding a small doctor's bag got out.

"Dr. Madsen. Good evening," said the inspector. "Now if you'll excuse me, Lady Dorothea."

"Of course." But she had no intention of leaving. She wanted to talk to the doctor when he had finished his observation of the body.

Dr. Madsen lifted his hat as he passed into the darkness and followed the inspector to the back of the stables.

"How are you holding up?" Dodo asked Rupert. "Wish I had some brandy for you."

"I'm fine. I just can't believe it. Rafe wouldn't hurt a fly. Ask anyone." He began to pace.

"Didn't you say he was recently single? What was that all about?"

"Florence Tingey. Lady Florence actually. Heard of her?"

"In spite of popular opinion to the contrary, the aristocracy is not some secret club where we all get together at weekends," she retorted.

Rupert crumpled some more. *Not the time for levity.*

"I'm so sorry, darling. Tactless of me. You've had a terrible shock." She pulled him close. "No. I've never heard of her."

"She is a fourth cousin of the king. Very la-di-da. She met Rafe in Italy about a year ago. Holiday romance kind of thing. Hierarchies and the like don't seem to matter as much on holiday, do they? Anyway, Rafe was besotted. I've never seen him like that. She was a tiny little blonde thing with a wicked sense of humor and they had such fun. But when they returned to England her ardor seemed to diminish and then someone caught her in a compromising position with another man. Rafe was shattered. Turns out the other chap was a marquess; much more suitable for a relative of the king than a mere earl, or so he thought. To save her reputation, Rafe did the chivalrous thing and broke it off."

23

Dodo knew all too well the hierarchy within the nobility. But it was 1924! "If she would throw him over for that, she wasn't good enough for him, anyway."

Dodo cast about for a change of subject. "What about the chaps from the other team. Did you know any of them? You said one of them was peeved about Rafe's gloating."

"As a matter of fact, I did. I've even played on the same team with one of them—years ago. Robert Dalrymple. Nice chap. Then there was Max Fortnon. The one who yelled at Rafe. He's *not* such a nice fellow. Notorious for making illegal fouls during games. You remember him, he's the one that made me drop my mallet—which is not a foul. The other two players were new to me."

"Could this Max have got into an argument with Rafe when he went back to the stables after we all left?"

"It's possible. He's a thoroughly vicious reprobate."

Dodo made a mental note to see if her friend David Bellamy knew any gossip about this Max fellow.

"What did Rafe do when he was not playing polo?"

"He tried university for a while, but sons who will inherit a fortune have less motivation than other chaps. He didn't graduate."

"His father is deceased, obviously," she commented. "When did that happen? He must have been relatively young." Keeping Rupert's mind off the body of his friend was her main concern at this point.

"Yes, about five years ago, now. Right at the end of the war."

"Was it natural causes?" she asked as the horses grunted and nickered nearby, obviously recognizing their owner's voice.

"I think so. I was still in France trying to save the war horses. I didn't make it to the funeral and mail was not getting through."

That would bear investigation. So often murders were tied to something in the past.

Another forgettable car arrived, and a man in a dirty mackintosh stepped out holding a camera with a flash. His eyes bulged as he got a view of glamorous Dodo among the hay and dung of the yard.

"In there?" he asked them in a gruff voice, his eyes following the line of Dodo's bespoke gown.

Dodo nodded, and he was swallowed by the darkness of the barn. Within moments bright flashes appeared in the back. She would like to get hold of those pictures when they were developed.

Rupert began to pace again, and Dodo left him to his thoughts keeping an eye out for the doctor. Before long, yet another vehicle arrived and two officers holding a stretcher jumped out and hurried into the interior of the barn. The pool of cars was getting deep as the first fingers of dawn crept over the horizon.

Dodo's spine tingled as the stretcher reappeared, a sheet covering the body, and she glanced at Rupert who had stopped walking, haunted eyes fixed on the stretcher.

"May I—?" she asked with her most earnest smile.

The first of the two policemen, glanced back to where the invisible inspector stood, a frown of concern wrinkling his young brow. "I don't know…"

"He need not know if we are quick," she encouraged. "Just a peek."

Rupert was rooted to the spot. She touched his arm asking a question with her fingers. He turned to her still dazed but nodding slowly. She pulled the sheet up and Rupert's face totally collapsed in abject horror. She dropped the sheet as her own stomach rolled.

The murderer had been in quite a passion.

Chapter 4

Needing some air, Dodo guided Rupert out of the yard. His wet cheeks reflected the early morning light.

"How awful," she gasped. In all the cases she had worked on, there had been little physical evidence of the crime. The sight of poor Rafe had made her insides churn.

The doctor stepped into the dewy courtyard.

"Oh, Dr. Madsen. Excuse me," she said running over to him.

He looked up, his face displaying the combined horrors of many years as a coroner. "Yes?"

"I wonder…we are friends of the deceased. Is there anything you can tell us?"

He stopped and dragged a hand down his careworn face. "Nasty business. Nasty business." He shook his head as though even he had found this crime to be particularly violent. "Friends, you say? It wasn't a friend who did *that* to him. Bludgeoned repeatedly with the mallet that was next to the body. The only good news I have is that he never saw it coming. In my expert opinion, he was dead from the initial blow. The first hit was on the back of the head."

"You don't think he suffered, then?" she asked.

"I would surmise that he died instantly, but I will confirm that during the autopsy."

"Thank you, doctor."

He shuffled to his car.

"Still here?" The thorny inspector came up behind them.

"Yes, I—we wanted to speak to the doctor."

"Strong blow to the back of the head. Would take the strength of a man in my estimation, though a strong woman might succeed."

Dodo merely nodded, hoping that the inspector might reveal other clues.

The yard was concrete strewn with bits of hay, dirt, and mud tracked across it by horses, grooms, and riders. The inspector kicked the dirt with his boot. "Too many footprints to be any use, but no marks made by a lady's heels." The inspector was clearly not a fan of the sport and did not know that most of the ladies wore the unflattering, flat wellington boots.

"Either of you smoke?" he asked, the unlit pipe clamped between his teeth.

"No, it makes me cough," Dodo explained.

"What about the other people on your team?" he asked.

"Rupert?" Dodo turned to him.

"Rafe didn't. He tried it at school for a dare, and it made him sick for hours. Never touched cigarettes again. Hugh doesn't as far as I'm aware, but Jasper has been known to smoke the odd cigar."

"What about the ladies?" asked the inspector.

Rupert pressed his lips together in concentration. "Juliette does not, Rosamund occasionally."

"What about Poppy?" asked Dodo.

"I really don't know. We've just met." Rupert scratched his scrubby chin and murmured, "Florence."

The inspector cocked an ear. "Yes?"

"She is Rafe's ex. She smoked all the time, reeked of it…but she wasn't even here."

The inspector pulled something from his pocket with a handkerchief and placed it in his open palm. A black matchbook with the emblem of a gold serpent embossed on the front, shone in the dawn light.

Dodo did not recognize the logo.

"Could be the brand of a jazz club or upscale pub," said Rupert. "I don't recognize it."

The inspector slipped it back into his pocket.

"Were you with each other the whole time yesterday after the tea party broke up?"

Dodo caught Rupert's eye. "Rupert dropped me off at my hotel and he went to Rafe's aunt's house, where they were staying. He came to pick me up two hours later."

"What time would that have been?" asked the inspector.

"Between five and seven o'clock. Our reservation was at half past seven," she explained.

27

"Did anyone see either of you during that time?"

"I booked a bath on my return and one of the chamber maids accompanied me," said Dodo. "That was at half past five. I left the bathroom about a quarter past six, oh, and I ordered some tea at half past six. I spent the rest of the time in my room getting ready."

The inspector turned his attention to Rupert.

"Rafe's aunt was in when I returned. I had a bath too, which the servants prepared. I don't keep a valet, so I bathed myself. That would have been between half past five and six o'clock. Rafe's aunt sent a maid to ask if I was staying for dinner at about half past six. Then I got dressed and said a quick goodbye to his aunt before I raced out around ten minutes to seven to pick up Dodo from the hotel."

Dodo had an idea. "May I ask what Rafe was wearing?" The sheet had only revealed his damaged head.

"Tan slacks, a navy-blue polo club blazer with a red and white crest on the pocket, and a white shirt with a blue and yellow cravat."

Exactly what all four of them had been wearing at tea. Rafe had never left the club!

"Thank you, inspector."

"Now, I can see you are both done in, but I shall need to question you further. Where can I reach you?"

Dodo wrote down the telephone number of her hotel and handed the notebook to Rupert.

"I can't go back," he groaned. "I'm staying with Rafe's aunt. I cannot impose at such a time."

"You're probably right. I'm sure they have rooms at my hotel," she assured him. "You can send for your things later."

Rupert handed back the pad and the grumpy inspector touched his hat. "Till later then. By the way, the name's Bradford."

Sometimes prone to nightmares, Dodo was wrenched awake as a bloody Rafe swung at her with a polo mallet. Heart hammering in her chest, her breathing short and shallow, she squinted as the sun poured through the gap in the curtains. Putting a hand to her damp brow, she reached for the glass of water on the bedside table.

It had been after six in the morning when she and Rupert had arrived at the hotel and half an hour later by the time they sorted out a room for him and got settled. It had taken her another half an hour to uncoil from the disturbing events of the evening and drop off. A glance at the clock told her it was just before one in the afternoon. Her mouth felt like a burr.

Her first reaction was to ring for Lizzie, but she had not accompanied Dodo on this trip. She was in Devon meeting her young man, Ernie's, parents. Dodo struggled out of bed and searched for her toothbrush. The bite of the new mint paste slapped her awake and she leaned on the small sink in her room, peering into the mirror. Her eyes were pink and her raven hair a wreck. Thank goodness for hats. *Hats!* Where on earth had she left her French creation from last night? It must still be outside the stable at the polo club or in the taxi.

Inspector Bradford had left a message to pay him a visit at the police station in Wexford at their earliest convenience, so after calling Hugh and Jasper to fill them in on what they had learned the previous night, they traveled over and were now seated in a converted mill, waiting to be interviewed. It was a pretty, whitewashed building with pots of tulips flanking the entrance and the pleasant sound of the river bubbling by. The inactive mill wheel itself had been preserved and took up a large portion of the waiting room.

An older lady in a battered hat and bandaged wrist had come to report that her cat was missing, and another woman with a face like a lemon had arrived to bail out her drunk of a husband. She didn't look too pleased to get him back.

"Lady Dorothea Dorchester?" A tall officer with a scar by his nose was reading from a clipboard. She raised her hand. "If you will kindly follow me?"

She squeezed Rupert's hand and followed the officer through to a narrow corridor and into a pleasant room with floral curtains at the window. The grouchy inspector had several pictures on his desk of a large family and what looked like several grandchildren. There were fresh narcissus in a metal jug on a table near the window that filled the air with their scent. It was a far cry from Scotland Yard.

"Biccie?" He offered her a plate full of delicious looking, homemade shortbread biscuits. If she hadn't just eaten, she would have readily taken one.

"That is very kind of you, Inspector, but I am full from a hearty lunch."

He leaned back in his chair, arms behind his head, lips pulled to the right. "I checked up on you."

"I am happy to hear it, Inspector."

"Inspector Hornby couldn't speak highly enough of you." He leaned forward reaching a pointed finger across his desk. "That don't mean I want you on my case, you understand. We do things differently out in the country. You let me do my job, and I'll turn a blind eye if you do a little snooping on the side."

"That is very gracious of you, Inspector." A hint of a smile tugged at her lips.

"Now that's understood, how well did you know Mr. Alleyn?"

"Not at all. I met him for the very first time after the polo match," she explained.

"Oh, I thought he was good friends with your young man."

"He was, but I have only been seeing Rupert since November and I had not met Rafe yet."

"What do you know about him?"

Dodo told him all that Rupert had revealed to her the night before.

The inspector picked up his pipe and clenched it between yellow teeth. "His father died, you say? Do you know how?"

"I don't. It happened during the war when communication was difficult. But…"

Leaning forward, his bushy brows raised, he said, "Go on."

30

"I have been involved in several cases where the motive stemmed from the past. It would be worth checking into."

He took a puff. "Do you happen to know what Lord Alleyn did in the war?"

"I'm sorry I don't, but I'm sure Rupert can fill you in."

A sharp knock on the door gave Dodo a start.

"Go away! I'm interviewing," he growled.

His smile was as weak as twice-used tea bags. "Sorry about that. Now, what about the other people in the party? Did there seem to be any ill will between any of them?"

"Quite the opposite, Inspector. Everyone was riding high from the win, as far as I could tell. Well, that is among the young people. Lady Boynton seemed out of sorts but then she may be that way all the time. I'd never met her before."

"I'll be interviewing everyone, so I can see for myself." He shuffled through some paperwork.

"Rupert did mention a connection with the other team," she added.

"Oh, yes?" The inspector tipped his wiry head to the side, the spitting image of an Alsatian.

"Two of the players were known to Rupert and perhaps by default Rafe, and one had a nasty temper, by all accounts. Max someone. He's not above cheating, apparently."

"I'll ask Mr. Danforth about him." He jotted down the name. "I checked your alibi with the hotel staff this morning, and they have confirmed your account. If you can think of nothing else, that will be all for now."

Dodo walked to the door. "There is one more thing that could be something or nothing. If you remember, Rupert mentioned that Rafe had recently broken off a relationship with a girl. Might be some bad blood there?"

"Do you happen to remember her name?"

"Florence. Can't remember her last name but she is a fourth cousin to the king."

The inspector's shaggy brows jiggled.

"Aren't you lovely?" smiled the stooped old lady through a mouth full of gaps.

"Thank you!" said Dodo, graciously. Thinking the town must be quite small, she asked, "I don't suppose you know a Lady Milton?"

"Know her lovey? I'm her dairy maid." She clasped the injured wrist. "Why d'you ask?"

Should Dodo mention the murder? No. It wasn't her place and it would be awful for gossip to pass round the town before Rafe's aunt had been informed.

"My boyfriend has been staying with Lady Milton for a few days. He knows her nephew."

"You must be talking about Master Rafe. I remember him as a boy. Sweet little fellow he was. Do you know he once climbed a tree to rescue my cat? Not the one that's missing. My old cat. But he did get up to mischief at times." She rolled her rheumy eyes. "What you doing here, then?"

"I had to make a statement to the police," Dodo explained.

"Posh girl like you getting into trouble?" The old lady frowned, disparaging wrinkles rippling across her features.

"No, no! It's nothing like that," Dodo protested. "I am a witness."

"Witness?" croaked the old girl.

Dodo patted the side of her nose. "Something a bit, hush, hush."

The old lady dipped her chin and winked a wrinkled eye.

"Mrs. Crackling," said the desk sergeant waving a paper. "I found that form for you to fill out about your missing cat."

The old lady's baggy mouth pulled down in a shrug and Dodo realized she couldn't read.

"Would you like me to help with that since your wrist is bandaged." She pointed to the spotless white fabric that was poking out from the bottom of Mrs. Crackling's grubby coat sleeve.

The cloudy eyes glanced down as if seeing the bandage for the first time. "Oh, that would be right nice of you."

Dodo took the form from the policeman. "Now, what is your cat's name?"

32

For the next several minutes they filled out the paperwork together, Dodo's mind only half on the task as she wondered how Rupert was holding up.

As she handed the form back to the sergeant, Rupert appeared looking ghostly white.

"All done?"

He nodded.

"I was just helping Mrs. Crackling file a report about her cat."

Rupert nodded a robotic greeting.

"Let's get you some food," Dodo said guiding him to the door before he mentioned Rafe. "Goodbye."

Once on the street she grabbed Rupert's arm. "You look awful. What happened?"

"With every passing minute the reality of what has happened to Rafe hits deeper. How does a chap survive a wretched war and then end up being killed like that in his prime?"

Spotting a tea shop, Dodo pulled Rupert in and ordered for them both settling at a window table as Rupert stared mindlessly through the glass.

"Did the inspector's questions dredge up some bad memories?"

"You could say that. I had quite forgotten that Rafe's father was a brutal disciplinarian. When he came back for a new term at school, he usually had some new bruises and marks. He was the only one who liked school better than home. He would beg me to take him back with me to *Knightsbrooke Priory* for the holidays. The stories he would tell." Rupert shuddered.

"I'm so sorry. What about his mother?"

"Lady Alleyn was a gentle soul who hardly dared speak against her husband. I imagine she was relieved when he died."

A jolly waitress brought their tea and Rupert stirred it absentmindedly.

"Please don't take this the wrong way…but who inherits now?" asked Dodo.

With effort, Rupert's faraway gaze narrowed in on her. "I hadn't considered that. Some cousin, I suppose."

"It might be worth finding out and while we're at it, discover how his father died."

Rupert's blue eyes bulged. "You think this might be tied to the past?"

"Murder often is," she affirmed, adding a spoonful of sugar to her cup. "And do you think Florence bore him any ill will?"

Rupert brandished his teaspoon like a baton. "If anything, it would have been the other way round. She treated him very badly."

"There's usually two sides to every story. It's worth looking into."

"I want you to work on this, Dodo," whispered Rupert urgently, finally emerging from the fog of grief that had shrouded him. "We must get justice for Rafe."

"Are you prepared for the unintended consequences?" she asked. "You know it can be harrowing learning your friends' deepest secrets and flaws."

He hit the table spilling tea everywhere. "I owe it to Rafe. Let's do this!"

Chapter 5

J asper had an arm tightly around the charming Juliette, his eyes wary. The small country pub had high, dark benches and the four of them were tucked in a back corner, away from the locals who eyed them suspiciously.

"Have you been questioned yet?" Jasper asked Rupert. "That inspector pulls no punches. He all but accused me of the murder."

"Did he?" asked Rupert. "He was tough, but he didn't go so far as that."

Jasper grabbed his neck. "I had the misfortune of going back to the changing rooms right after we all split up—I'd forgotten my stupid wallet. While I was there, I overheard Rafe speaking to someone in urgent, hushed tones but I didn't give it a second thought as I was in a hurry. The inspector accused me of making up a mystery person and going back in to kill him. Me! One of his *best* friends." His hand dropped leaving white splotches on his red neck.

"I am not defending the inspector's tactics," began Dodo. "However, in a murder case, everyone is considered a suspect. It is in the courts that one is considered innocent until proven guilty."

Jasper grabbed Juliette's hand. "Well, it has thrown us for a loop. We just want to be left alone in our grief and the inspector comes along and pokes the hornet's nest."

"I quite understand," she sympathized. "How did you meet Rafe?"

"It was after the war. I met Rupert while we were in the service and when it was all over we stayed in touch. Knowing I had played polo, Rupert and Rafe talked about getting a team together. One of the chaps on the opposing team, Robert Dalrymple, was part of our original line up but he lived too far away, and it was difficult to get together to practice. In the end he decided to join another team. That's when we recruited Hugh. He was a friend of mine from school. That was what?" He looked at Rupert. "Four years ago."

"About that," said Rupert. "Interestingly enough, Rafe and Hugh had met before. I think they are loosely related by marriage."

"Do you get together socially, much?" she asked, watching condensation build up on Rupert's glass of beer.

Jasper relaxed his hold on Juliette. "Yes, but not since Rupert met you. He's been somewhat of a ghost." He glanced at Rupert who looked sheepish.

"Guilty," he said.

This piece of news was a bit of a reckoning. Dodo suddenly realized that since she and Rupert had met, they had become quite insular—any socializing had been with family or her friends. She thought back to her twenty-first birthday bash; she had not even considered asking him if he wanted to invite anyone. *How selfish she had been!* Jasper's words made her realize that Rupert had sacrificed time with his own set to be with her.

It was another reason to love him.

"I feel suitably honored," she purred, sending Rupert a shy smile.

"Well, the minute we met you we could all see why," said Juliette. "You are like two halves of the same whole!"

Dodo's cheeks tingled. "That is so sweet of you to say."

"And absolutely true," said Rupert kissing her cheek.

As much as she relished this welcome support from Rupert's friends, the principal reason for the get-together was to conduct a sly, informal interview of their own.

"Do you have any idea why Rafe went back to the stables?" she asked.

"I know one of his ponies had stumbled during the second chukka. He probably went to make sure all was well. He had a special affinity with his animals," suggested Jasper.

"That's right," agreed Rupert. "Maribelle did falter out on the field."

"Perhaps he saw something he shouldn't. Getting rid of witnesses is an occupational hazard of murderers." She ran a finger round the rim of her wine glass. "Jasper, you say you heard him talking to someone?"

"Yes, in the changing room. I couldn't hear what they were saying, and I was in a hurry to get back to Juliette."

"Male or female?"

36

Jasper lifted his eyes to the wooden beams on the ceiling. "Male I think, but it could have been a female with a low voice."

"That lets me out, then," said Juliette with a halfhearted laugh. "But now that we are talking about it, I saw someone come out of the changing rooms and rush inside the stable. I was waiting for Jasper by the tea tent and whoever it was, wore black with their head down. It was dusk, and I couldn't see very well."

"Where exactly were you waiting?" she asked Juliette.

"Just outside the entrance to the pavilion. A cold wind had whipped up and I was chilly. I remember because two of the waitresses got into a huge fight. Cat calling and scratching. The manager had to come and break it up. I joked with the captain—oh, I forgot! He came back to the tea tent, too. He was looking for one of his gloves."

The captain had returned? That was news. He was a cousin of Rafe's, wasn't he? Did he inherit?

"Was Rafe in any sort of trouble?" Rupert asked Jasper. "Did he say anything to you?"

"No—" Jasper stopped short. "He did call me on the telephone last week. He seemed rather down. Kept talking about Florence so I told him she wasn't worth it. Juliette thought he might like Poppy. That's why we invited her, as a matter of fact. She's a lovely girl and currently unattached and we hoped they might hit it off."

So many unanswered questions. Dodo needed to stop and buy a notebook at *Brown's*.

They arranged to meet Hugh and Rosamund for dinner, which gave them some time after lunch at the pub to rest before getting ready. Dodo took the time to write the things she had already learned in a new notebook. So many people had gone back to the polo grounds.

She checked her appearance in the mirror before running to meet Rupert. Not as good as Lizzie achieved but good enough until her maid returned.

The restaurant was all oak and buttoned leather, u-shaped benches that wrapped around heavy dark wood tables. The air was thick with smoke that hung like ghostly veils and Dodo hoped it wouldn't cause a coughing fit.

Hugh and Rosamund were already there and Hugh raised a hand. Rosamund wore a rust-colored gown which set off her russet hair perfectly. However, her face bore traces of strain and her eyes were rather dull. Hugh looked equally gloomy and Dodo remembered that Jasper had mentioned that Hugh was related to Rafe.

"How are you holding up?" Hugh asked Rupert, whose expression matched his own. "I think it would have broken me to see poor Rafe."

"It was pretty ruddy," Rupert admitted. "I shall try to erase the image from my memory and remember him hitting that last goal. He was ecstatic."

For several minutes they reminisced about the good times, announcing play-by-plays of old games as if they were calling the events on the radio.

"I can't believe he's gone," said Hugh finally.

"We heard you are related," Dodo said.

"Yes, it was rather funny, actually. He is only called Raphael in the family so when Jasper and Rupert approached me about joining their team and told me the other teammate's name, I had no idea it was him. It wasn't till we met that we stared at each other then laughed out loud."

"Were you close?" she asked.

"As children not particularly. My uncle is married to Rafe's mother's cousin. We are distant in-laws but we would see each other at weddings, funerals, and christenings. We'd get into scrapes when we were bored at such events. My mother said he was a bad influence. I'm sure his mother said the same about me. And we were the same age. We had become much closer recently as we played polo together."

Dodo saw Rosamund squeeze Hugh's hand.

"Did you know his father?" she asked him.

Hugh's mouth pulled down. "I only really knew him by reputation. A harsh man, by all accounts. I know once Rafe was sixteen, he rarely went home. Until his father died, that is. He was close to his mother. She will take it very hard."

"How were your interviews with the inspector?" asked Rupert. "He gave Jasper a bit of a hard time."

Hugh tilted his head with raised brows. "Did he?"

"Well, Jasper admitted to going back to the changing room for his wallet. He told the inspector he heard someone in a serious conversation with Rafe but didn't see who. The inspector accused him of making it up and of killing Rafe himself."

Hugh's face colored. "I say! That's a bit off! How dare he!"

"I think the inspector was just shaking the tree to see if anything fell," remarked Dodo. "He didn't do anything like that with you?"

"No. I would have pushed back, I can tell you." Hugh was getting into a lather.

"It's alright, darling," said Rosamund. "He's just doing his job." She looked across the table at Dodo. "He was actually quite pleasant to me."

"How long had *you* known Rafe?" Dodo asked Rosamund.

"They only met through me, last year," Hugh explained.

Rosamund cast nervous eyes at Hugh. "Actually..."

"Actually what?" Hugh's massive jaw tightened, and Dodo could see it working through his skin.

Bright red spots colored Rosamund's cheeks. "I met him at my cousin's birthday party when I was fourteen. Before the war."

"You never said." A harsh crease had formed between Hugh's eyes.

"Well, we hit it off and saw each other a few times. But it was nothing. Childhood stuff. And then the war came. When you first introduced us, Hugh, I didn't even recognize him. He was so changed. But he recognized me. We decided it wasn't worth mentioning."

The tension around the table was charged like ignited dynamite. "Why not? If it was all so innocent?" spat out Hugh.

"Because it was nothing and so long ago." Rosamund reached for Hugh's hand, but he snatched it away.

"I want you to promise never to keep anything from me in the future." Hugh's tone was dangerous, and Dodo felt herself stiffen.

Before her eyes, the dynamics shifted subtly as Rosamund refused to answer Hugh immediately. She waited, chin jutting forward as her nails scratched the tabletop. After several awkward minutes with Hugh glaring, she sneered, "Do you want a list of *all* my former boyfriends?"

Dodo gave Rupert the side eye. He shrugged.

"I am François, and I will be your waiter this evening." A thin waiter with a threadbare mustache and a fake French accent stood to attention like a culinary soldier, white towel over his arm, pencil poised.

"Go away," Hugh growled without taking his eyes off Rosamund who was holding his stare with a fierce expression.

The feeble waiter diminished like a burst bubble. "Of course! Of course! I shall come back later." He almost bent in half as he scurried away.

"All?" Hugh's voice was growing in volume and intensity. He was about to create a very public scene.

"You don't think we sat home knitting while you were all away at war, do you?" Rosamund scoffed.

"So, you spent your time with draft dodgers?" bellowed Hugh, which turned the heads of several other diners.

"Hugh, I was *fifteen* when the war started, for crying out loud. There were still plenty of boys around who were too young to serve."

Dodo pursed her lips. She and Rupert could do with a nice sink hole to open up and swallow them, right about now.

"So, you let everyone take a bite of you?" Hugh snarled.

From out of nowhere, Rosamund's hand came up and slapped Hugh right across the face. "This is exactly why Rafe and I didn't tell you. Because you are the jealous type."

The other guests had abandoned discretion and were fully engaged in the ongoing drama as Rosamund pushed back from the table and stormed out of the restaurant, leaving Dodo and Rupert alone with the humiliated Hugh. Dodo bit her lip.

His broad hand went slowly to his glowing cheek. But the slap seemed to have brought him to his senses.

"Idiot!" he cried. "She's right. I *am* a jealous fool. I can't seem to control it sometimes." He looked up, a new kind of frown on his face.

"We're all upset about Rafe and tensions are high. You'd better go after her," said Rupert. "Go man! She's the best thing that's ever happened to you."

Hugh slid around the bench and threw his napkin on the table. "You're right. Sorry. I completely ruined the evening."

"It's fine. Just go," said Rupert.

They watched as he ran out the door in search of Rosamund. A bubble of nervous laughter bounced around Dodo's chest until it tickled her throat and spilled out, triggering a similar response from Rupert. The laughter built until they were both howling hysterically, tears running down the sides of Dodo's cheeks.

Several minutes later, the nervous energy drained from their systems, they both slumped over the table, exhausted. From the corner of her eye, Dodo could see the rebuffed waiter approaching like a rejected lover.

She lifted her head.

"I am François—"

The wild, uncontrollable laughter attacked them again.

Chapter 6

"**D**odo!" David Bellamy cried into the telephone. She held the earpiece away from her head. The sounds of yet another party came through the line. "Haven't seen you since your birthday bash. How the dickens are you?"

"I'm fine David. Is this a bad time?" She could hear a girl twittering in the background.

"It's never a bad time when you call, darling. You should know that by now." David was an incurable flatterer, but his comment made Dodo smile.

"What can I do for you, sweetheart? Throwing another memorable party? Is Rupert hosting an SJP?" He was referring to Rupert's thriving business of organizing large, secret jazz bashes around London. They'd been given the acronym SJP by attendees. Dodo had yet to attend one.

"No. Nothing like that I'm afraid."

There was a short pause at the other end and Dodo could imagine David's charismatic face transformed by a wicked grin. "You're embroiled in another murder, aren't you?" It was an accusation.

"Possibly."

"I knew it!" he crowed into the telephone line. "How can I help?"

Dodo told him about Rupert's polo teammate being murdered and the fellow, Max, on the opposing team who was reputed to have a nasty temper. "So, I need you to put your ear to the ground and see what you can find out about Max Fortnon."

"Like Fortnon and Martin's, the fancy food emporium?" he asked.

"Yes, just like that."

"No problem. That all?"

"Since you are offering," she responded. "The deceased, Raphael Alleyn, had recently broken up with one Lady Florence Tingey. I understand she is loosely related to the king. My path has never crossed hers. I believe she behaved badly, and he broke off the

42

relationship in a show of gallantry. I'm wondering if she wanted her cake and to eat it too and things turned ugly."

"Juicy."

"And there is one more, if you are up to the task." She knew he would not be able to resist. Rumor was the spice of his life.

"You know me and gossip, darling—like mud on a pig."

She grinned. "Rafe had a cousin that came to the polo game on Saturday. He's in the army. He seems extremely honorable and nice, but Rafe was an only child and I'm wondering if the captain is now the heir."

"Suspicious. I love it! Let me grab a piece of paper to write these names down or I'm sure to forget. Hold on!"

"Hello!" panted a girl in a high, vague voice somewhere between the tone of a toddler and an adolescent. "Who are *you*?"

"Well, who are *you*?" Dodo responded in kind.

"I'm Priscilla." She laid heavy emphasis on the middle syllable and snickered.

Dodo rolled her eyes. "This is Princess Mary."

A shriek and a hiccup could be heard as the telephone receiver crashed to the tabletop. Dodo winced.

"Dodo?"

"David, the intelligence quotient of your girlfriends seems to get lower and lower."

"Well, the most intelligent girl I know rebuffed me. What was I supposed to do?" *Zing!*

"Touché. But try for a little more between the ears in future."

"'Cilla's fun with few demands. And you have no moral grounds to reprimand me, darling. You're the one who broke my heart."

She knew this was only half true. "Ready for the names?"

The tea shop was a classy place with a modern, art deco exterior and large windows. She pushed through the door and found herself in a Hollywood-style room with steel and glass tables and s-shaped chairs. The waitresses were dressed in red satin gowns with red and white striped aprons. Every one of them wore their hair in a modern

43

bob. It was a far cry from the tea shop in Little Puddleton. She would have to bring her sister, Didi.

Scanning the room, she spotted Juliette wearing a dashing purple hat, silk roses trailing across the brim. She raised her hand in welcome. As expected, Poppy was sitting beside her.

"What a fabulous place!" Dodo gasped as she sat at a table already laden with delicious cakes and pastries. Neither girl had one on her plate.

"Not eating?" she asked.

"I've had no appetite since poor Rafe died," said Juliette with a sigh.

Poppy stared at the pastries and then at Dodo with a mouth shrug. Dodo mirrored her expression and refrained from taking one.

Thrilled when Juliette called and suggested they go out for tea with Poppy, Dodo had hoped to start the afternoon off with small talk, then bring the subject around to the murder. But the topic had been dropped right into her lap.

"Yes, Rupert is incredibly upset. He's popped up to Essex to give his condolences to Rafe's mother in person. She's all alone now."

"That's so nice of him," said Poppy, dropping more cubes of sugar into her tea.

"I understand you were being set up with Rafe that day," Dodo said, pouring tea from a plain, white ceramic teapot on the table into the strainer.

Poppy's face lit up like the waitress's dresses. "Oh, gosh! You know about that? Seems such a faux pas now. But Juliette explained that Rafe had been a bit down since breaking it off with Lady Florence. I'm currently single and thought, why on earth not? You know?" She stirred her tea. "A chap who has the seal of approval of one of your best friends is better than meeting a random fellow at a party or something. And an earl to boot."

Dodo couldn't agree more. "I should say!"

"And he was a lovely man," said Juliette in a quiet voice. "So often those who are treated badly as a child turn out rough themselves but not Rafe. All the boys love their horses, but Rafe took their care to a new level. That's why he went back to the stable

44

that day, to check on one of them. Maribelle, I think. He cared so much about them." She swiped at her cheek. "If he hadn't, he might still be alive."

"That was the first time you had met him?" Dodo asked Poppy.

"Yes. I watched him play, of course, and then we were introduced in the tea tent. I thought him a very handsome man and knowing what I did from Juliette, I thought we might hit it off. I must say he seemed to like me too. He kept catching my eye over tea and even whispered in my ear that he was looking forward to dinner with pleasure, before we all scattered. I was excited about the possibilities."

"How long had you known Rafe?" she asked Juliette, who was still struggling to control her emotions.

"I actually met him first," Juliette explained. "I was watching a polo game my cousin was playing in, and Rafe and the boys were on the opposing team. After the game, my team's supporters all went to a local pub where Rafe's lot had ended up. I went to the bar for a refill and Rafe was standing there. He thought the glass the bar tender put down was the one he had ordered and we both went for it at the same time. He apologized profusely, and I said it was fine and asked if he was one of the players, which I already knew, of course. We chatted for a bit and then I went back to my table but every time I looked up, Rafe was looking in my direction." She fingered her napkin. "I saw this other chap teasing him about not paying attention to their conversation—it was Jasper. Before Rafe left the pub, he got my name and number.

"We went out for a few dates but in spite of that initial attraction, we both knew there was no romantic spark. We were more like good friends. But Jasper was always around, and I didn't know that he liked me until Rafe and I decided to split up and Jasper asked if Rafe would mind if he tried for me. I had felt an attraction to him from early on but didn't think that was fair to Rafe, so I didn't act on it."

Well, well, well.

This explained why Juliette was so cut up about Rafe's death.

"Rafe, being the sweet chap he was, had no problem with it, and Jasper and I have been inseparable ever since. I really thought he was going to propose the night of the—well, you know."

Poppy slipped a cake onto her plate and broke off a little piece. "So, you see, there was no better recommendation. An ex-girlfriend who sang his praises." When Juliette looked down, she popped it into her mouth.

"What about Hugh and Rosamund?" Dodo asked.

Juliette fiddled with her teacup. "They met at Epsom during the Royal Races. Their families were both invited to a private box. He was smitten immediately but the way she tells it, Rosamund took a little longer to see the light. They met shortly after Jasper and I started courting."

"Rupert was the only single one?"

Juliette slid her eyes to Dodo. "What makes you think he was single?"

The comment was like a punch to Dodo's gut. She and Rupert had skirted the topic of former girlfriends but Rupert hadn't been very specific.

"Assuming is never a good idea," Dodo said with a nervous laugh.

"Oh, Rupert was never with one girl for very long. I don't remember him being serious about anyone before you, but look at the man. He's like some movie star. Then a few months ago, he disappeared off the map. We thought he might be ill or something. He never had time for us anymore. It was Jasper who guessed he had found a girl to tame him. I wasn't so sure. But I was wrong." She flashed her eyes up to meet Dodo's. "We were all very interested to meet the girl who had managed to catch Rupert Danforth."

Hearing about yourself in the third person was fraught with danger—it could go both ways. Dodo hadn't spent much time wondering what his friends thought about her. Perhaps she should have.

"Juliette was dying to meet you," revealed Poppy. "She thought you must be something ravishing to—"

"Poppy!" cried Juliette.

For the first time in a long while, Dodo felt a little self-conscious.

"Well, you were," Poppy repeated. She turned to face Dodo. "And you are! You're ideally suited, the pair of you. It's plain for anyone to see."

"Thank you," Dodo said, taking a sip of tea to process the girl's candor. "What do you think of Hugh and Rosamund as a couple?"

Juliette's delicate face hardened. "Why? What have you heard?"

Was she being defensive or curious? Dodo couldn't tell.

"It's just that we were out to dinner with them and they had a little...tiff."

"Really?" said Poppy, breaking off another chunk of the pastry.

"Oh, they do that all the time," assured Juliette, her expression showing disappointment. "Hugh has a rotten temper. Rosamund seems to know how to handle him though."

"What was the fight about?" Poppy was leaning forward, her necklace almost draping in her tea.

"Did you know that Rosamund and Rafe met when they were young?" Dodo announced.

Juliette dropped her teacup onto the saucer with a clink. "What?"

"Yes, it came up last night. She was only fourteen at the time. It was before the war and they only saw each other a few times. Then he went off to fight and they lost touch. When they met again, he was so changed she didn't recognize him right away."

"What about him? Did he recognize *her*?" asked Poppy.

"Yes, as a matter of fact. However, they decided their short relationship was so long ago and so insignificant, that neither of them would mention it. I guess by then Rosamund knew about Hugh's temper and asked Rafe to keep quiet about it. But now that Rafe has passed away, Rosamund felt she should say something."

"Well, I never!" said Juliette. "No wonder Hugh was angry. I can't believe it. Rafe had dated both of us. What were the chances?"

"It does make for a rather tangled web," Dodo agreed.

"What happened at the restaurant?" asked Poppy. "After Rosamund came clean?"

47

"To be honest, Hugh lost control." Dodo paused. "Rosamund slapped him."

Both girls snorted.

"It brought Hugh to his senses and he ran after her," Dodo explained. "But it was terrifically awkward for Rupert and I."

"What an interesting introduction to Rupert's inner circle you've had," said Juliette. "I swear there is not usually this much drama." She seemed to remember what had happened and her face filled with shame. "And here we are gossiping, when poor Rafe—" she descended into tears again and Poppy rubbed her shoulder.

"I should go," said Dodo feeling like an outsider. She had missed lunch and her stomach was growling with hunger pangs as she stared at the forbidden, sweet delicacies before her. She grabbed her clutch and shoved in a cake. Then wishing them both farewell, she threaded her way to the door.

As Dodo made her exit, she looked back. Juliette was still weeping, Poppy comforting her. Neither one had begged her to stay.

Chapter 7

D odo was back home at Beresford House in the cozy drawing room with her mother and father, when Rupert entered, fresh from his trip to Essex, looking anything but chipper.

"Darling!" she said at the very same time her mother said, "Rupert! So lovely to see you."

He stooped to give her mother, Guinevere, a kiss on the cheek and to shake Lord Dorchester's hand. "Good evening, sir."

"Good to see you, Rupert. Drink?"

"I'll take some brandy, if you have any," he replied and went to sit by Dodo. "Hello, sweetheart! You're a sight for sore eyes."

She snuggled into his side and whispered. "How was Rafe's mother?"

"To tell the truth she's in such a state, she can barely function. Life had finally changed for the better after her husband died. She was no longer under his thumb, and Rafe had come home. They'd become really close. And now this."

"Is there anyone to take care of her?" asked Dodo.

Dodo's father came over with a drink then went back to sit by his wife.

Fortunately, the aunt I stayed with for the polo is her sister. She's quite a bit younger and has come to stay. Good job or I think Lady Alleyn might do something awful to herself. The sister is organizing the funeral and running the house."

"Well, that's a blessing. Did Lady Alleyn speak to you at all?"

"Yes, but it unnerved me because the few times she did speak, she would talk about Rafe in the present tense, as if he were going to stride through the door at any moment. Her sister would just shrug about the behavior."

"How bizarre! But I suppose grief and shock affect people in many ways." Dodo remarked. "Did you manage to ferret out anything useful?"

49

"Lady Alleyn did inadvertently reveal that Rafe was stressed about something. He had expressed frustration but would not share with her what the problem was. He just kept saying that she needn't worry about it."

"Curious." Dodo ran a finger across his bottom lip and he playfully caught her finger between his teeth.

"She also rambled about the past and the present," he said, "mixing them up constantly. My head was spinning but quite by accident she also relayed that Rafe had uncovered the urgent need for extensive repairs and modernization to the house, for which they did not have sufficient funds."

"Is that a surprise to you?" Dodo asked.

"It is, yes. Rafe never talked about money. Inheriting an earldom can go both ways, in my experience. You either inherit a fortune that has been nicely managed by your forefathers or you find a bunch of debts awaiting you and not enough money to cover them. Sounds like for Rafe, it was the latter."

She laid her head on Rupert's shoulder. "Could this pressing need for funds have led to his death, do you think?"

"Aren't you always telling me that money is the strongest motive for murder?" He ran a finger down her nose and she shivered with pleasure, catching her father's disapproving eye.

"I think it's a starting point," she said. "When is the funeral?"

"The fourteenth. I shall attend, of course. Do you want to go? You don't have to. You only met him briefly."

She sat up. "Certainly. Out of support for you and the team and…for intelligence gathering."

He shifted away from her slightly. "I'm feeling a mixture of emotions about all this," he said quietly so as not to alert her parents. "When you were helping Beatrice because she had been wrongfully accused of murder, or uncovering who had murdered Granny, it was different. This time I feel like I'm on the other side from you. It feels…dirty."

Dirty?

She felt the word like an upper cut to the chin.

Managing a weak smile though she was dreadfully hurt, she asked, "Are you saying you want to leave this one to the police?" She found herself holding her breath, the answer pivotal.

His chest expanded against her in an enormous sigh. "I don't know, Dodo. I've thought of little else on the drive here."

"I'll leave it alone if you want me to?" she said, a sense of dread and fear worming its way into her chest.

He grabbed her hand and put his face close to hers. "These are my best friends and an investigation will reveal their dark sides, their deepest secrets. Things they don't voluntarily share. I'm not sure I want to know any of that." He rested his forehead against hers. "And I don't want any of this to become a wedge between us." He dropped his voice even lower. "Dodo, I love you desperately, but these are the kind of matters that ruin relationships."

"We're off, then," said her father in a gruff voice as her mother pulled him out the door. "Goodnight."

Dodo hardly registered his words.

What was Rupert saying?

"I'll stop," she said, placing her palms on his face. "Nothing is more important to me than you. I don't want anything to spoil that." She felt vulnerable, exposed. Frightened. They were meant to be together and anything that put that at risk was not worth it.

"I won't attend the funeral. Like you said, I didn't really know Rafe, and I'll be an outsider imposing on your team's private grief."

"Are you sure, darling?" He was searching her eyes with such pain and concern that she felt her own eyes swimming. He brushed at a tear that fell over her lid.

"I'm sure."

At breakfast the next morning, Sanderson entered the room with his usual invisibility.

"A telephone call for Lady Dorothea."

Lady Dorchester had readied a room for Rupert the night before and insisted that he stay. Dodo glanced at him across the table and cracked a smile before following Sanderson from the room.

51

"Dodo?"

David! Drat! She needed to call off the dogs.

"David, you're up early."

"I haven't gone to bed yet, dearest. We had a swinging time last night. But as luck would have it, someone mentioned your Lady Florence, so I mined them for information."

Dodo pursed her lips. "I'm dropping my investigation, David."

The line went so quiet she thought he had hung up on her.

"David?"

"I'm here. I'm just completely dumbstruck. Now I know I don't stand a chance."

"What makes you say that?" she asked.

"Only true love would induce you to drop a case."

She considered his comment as her mind and stomach swirled. He was right.

"This one hits too close to home. Rupert feels wrong about digging up muck about his friends behind their backs. It's too intrusive."

"Honor. Another stellar quality I can't possibly compete with."

"He's at a moral crossroads, David. I was worried I was going to lose him for a moment. I value him far too much to risk it."

David went quiet again. "You're going to marry him, darling. Mark my words. And if you're the bride, who will be my guest for the illustrious event?"

Chapter 8

A fter a long, heartfelt hug, Dodo asked, "So, how did things go?"

Lizzie was styling Dodo's hair and she saw a rosy color on her maid's cheeks reflected in the mirror.

"Ernie's mother and father are lovely—salt of the earth folks. His father was a laborer until Ernie became a valet and earnt enough to send money home so that his father could retire. Only—"

Dodo's eyes snapped up to meet her maid's.

"Only now that his employer has passed away, he will need to find new employment."

Words of consolation filled Dodo's brain as she recalled what Rupert had said about taking on a valet, at her birthday party. It was such a perfect solution she could almost squeal but it was not her secret to share, so she held her tongue.

"Less and less gentleman require a valet these days," Lizzie continued. "He's sent out lots of letters but not got many replies and even fewer interviews."

"I would hope there is always good work for an exceptional candidate," said Dodo carefully.

"Those gentleman that still use valets, already have good men, as they've had the pick of the crop." She turned to walk to the wardrobe. "But I've nothing but admiration for Ernie's work ethic and humility. He's been working as a waiter rather than let the grass grow under his feet."

"How very enterprising." Dodo swung around on the padded stool. "And I'm not surprised his parents welcomed you with open arms. Who wouldn't?"

"M'lady, you're making me blush." Brushing a boiled wool jacket she carried on. "They were so nice to me and kept winking at Ernie. They thought I wouldn't notice."

"Whereabouts in Devon do they live?"

"Not far from your cousins, as it happens. We took some strolls near the moors, but I told Ernie I had no desire to walk on them, not after all that fog when your cousin's young man was killed." Lizzie shivered.

The only saving grace from that blighted trip was that she had met Rupert. Dodo shuddered at the creepy memories. "I don't blame you at all."

"What did you do while I was gone, m'lady? How was the polo?"

Dodo slapped her knees. "You obviously haven't read the newspapers."

"What?" It was Lizzie's turn to catch Dodo's eye. "There's *not* been another murder?"

Dodo nodded, biting her lip. "One of Rupert's closest friends. A teammate. I had only just met him. Rupert is devastated."

"So how far have you got in the investigation?" Lizzie replaced the jacket in the white and gold art deco wardrobe.

"That's the thing. Rupert doesn't want me to investigate this. He says it feels wrong and underhanded to poke into his friend's lives."

Lizzie spun around, her eyes sharp. "I can appreciate that."

"So, out of respect for Rupert, I am leaving it alone."

Lizzie pursed her lips, face grim. "Please tell Mr. Danforth I am so sorry about his friend. Shall I ready your funeral clothes?"

Dodo swept her fringe out of her eyes. "No. I've decided not to go. I might not be able to help asking probing questions if I'm there. I didn't really know Rafe Alleyn, and I think I can support Rupert better by not going."

Rupert had already gone home to his little mews house in London to prepare for the funeral. He was going to stop back at Beresford House on his return journey.

Dodo rushed to hug her beloved maid again. "I've missed you so much!"

"It's good to be back," Lizzie responded. "I can see you're not your normal self. Has something else happened? Is there trouble between the two of you?"

Sinking onto the bed, Dodo tapped the coverlet for Lizzie to sit. "I was under the impression our relationship was strong enough to weather any storm," Dodo admitted. "But I was naive. We haven't actually been together very long, and this is a strong wave. Lizzie, I'm scared."

Lizzie took her by the shoulders. "It's healthy to have relationships tested," she assured her. "Look at Ernie and me. We can't plan for the future until he has a steady job. But I love him enough to wait any length of time. Obstacles can strengthen love."

"But what if *our* relationship isn't strong enough?"

"Nonsense!" said Lizzie. "By not attending the funeral and not investigating the murder you are showing respect for Mr. Danforth's feelings. When it's all over, he'll thank you for that and your relationship will be even stronger. You mark my words."

"You are so wise, Lizzie."

"It's because I come from a large family." She patted Dodo's arm. "Now, when is Miss Didi due back?"

Dodo clapped her hands together. "She's arriving tonight. I'm excited to hear how meeting Charlie's parents as his girlfriend, all went. Just like you, meeting Ernie's family."

Charlie Chadwick, an old family friend, was a post-graduate student and had a break between the end of Hilary and Trinity terms. He and Didi had traveled to his family's estate in the country. Dodo was dying to hear all about it.

After lots of shrieks and hugs, Didi fell back on Dodo's bed with her arms stretched high above her head.

"That good?" asked Dodo, content to see her younger sister so happy even if her own feelings were frayed.

Didi rolled over onto her stomach, legs bent at the knees, ankles crossed. "Better!"

"They loved you!" declared Dodo.

"I was subject to his older brother's family as well, and yes. Do you remember him? My memories were of a somewhat boring fellow, but he has grown up to be rather nice. There was just one little hiccup—his grandmother knows Granny, and they don't get along."

Dodo's grandmother was a stiff Edwardian who was surprisingly progressive, in certain things. Dodo was reminded of her recent interaction with Lady Boynton on the subject of Granny and could well imagine that not all of the dowager's encounters went swimmingly.

Dodo laughed. "That's not too much of a hurdle in the big scheme of things."

"Let's hope not!" Didi made a bridge for her chin with her hands. "I'm whipped, Dodo. When I am not with Charlie, I think about him all the time. I have no appetite and no desire to spend time with anyone else."

"I know that feeling," Dodo said with a weak grin.

"Perhaps there will be a double wedding," gushed Didi.

Dodo dropped to the bed. "Has Charlie proposed?"

"Not in so many words, but it's kind of understood. He wants to get this academic year under his belt, then there's just one more before he's earned his PhD. I told him he doesn't really need to work with my large dowry, but he says his pride won't let him live off my money. He's determined to make a living as a professor." She wrinkled her nose and clicked her shoes together. "I'm getting used to the idea of being a college professor's wife. I'm viewing it all as a grand adventure."

"Whoot, whoot!" Dodo chanted. "I am so happy for you, little sister."

"What about you? How was polo?" Didi asked, still prone on the bed.

Dodo dropped her eyes to the floor. "The polo was great but while you have been in heaven, there has been some violence down here on earth."

Didi pushed herself up on her arms, her face white. "Not Rupert?"

"No. No, of course not. I would have let you know. It was a teammate. One of Rupert's best friends. A lovely man called Rafe Alleyn."

"What happened?" Didi pulled her legs up to sit on the edge of the bed while Dodo took a seat in the armchair by the empty fireplace and filled her in.

"How awful!" cried Didi, reaching for her sister's hand.

"I know. It's really taken a toll on poor Rupert."

"I don't doubt it!" said Didi. "Who are the prime suspects?"

"It could have been anyone because we were in a public place," began Dodo.

"But…?"

"But it's likely one of the people associated with the team."

"You mean one of his friends." Didi's shapely brows crinkled. Dodo nodded.

"Who's at the top of your list?" asked Didi coming to crouch next to the chair.

"I don't have a list," Dodo said quietly.

Didi rocked back on her heels. "Don't have a list? Have the police warned you off?"

"Rupert doesn't want me to investigate." She explained his feelings on the matter.

"I suppose I can respect that," Didi said.

"Me too. So even though I had already set David some tasks, I've called him off."

Didi's pink lips twisted. "Rupert is worth it, Dodo."

"My thoughts exactly."

Dodo went to the window and looked out at their rolling land as the clouds scudded past like racing poodles. Heart heavy she needed distraction. "Have you spoken to Mummy yet?"

"She wasn't home. I came straight up here to you."

"Then let's see if she's back."

Dodo let her mind wander as Didi told her mother the details of her week away with Charlie and his family. They had gone for long walks, joined a hunt, punted on the lake of his family's estate and completed a huge jigsaw puzzle with Charlie's brother and his wife.

"Begging your pardon," croaked Sanderson in a voice so utterly posh it made the king sound common. "Lady Dorothea, Mr. Danforth is on the telephone."

She had been so distracted she had not noticed it ringing and hurried out to the telephone cabinet, her heart hammering. Closing the door, she grabbed the stick and earpiece, eager to hear Rupert's voice.

"Darling—"

She had hardly got the word out when Rupert interrupted her. "That idiot, Inspector Bradford, has arrested Hugh."

"Really?" She was shocked.

"I need you to do your thing." No small talk.

She hesitated. "How do you know it *wasn't* Hugh?"

"Call it instinct. There is no way it was Hugh. I simply know it wasn't, and I want you to prove it."

This was not the answer she hoped to hear. "I am happy to re-start my investigation but unless you have some concrete evidence that incriminates someone else, you have to accept that it *could* be Hugh and that my investigation could prove that."

"Do *you* suspect him?" Rupert's voice was rising with desperation.

"No, but the inspector must have some reason for arresting him," she pointed out. "What changed?"

"Someone saw him return to the stable area."

Dodo made a great effort to keep her voice level. "That is damning. Especially since he did not mention it in his statement. It means he lied to the police." *And us.* "Not good. Not good. Did he say why he returned?"

"He claims he did not and that the witness is mistaken." She heard Rupert exhale roughly through the line.

"Are you sure you want me to do this?" she asked, running a finger down the cold window of the telephone cabinet.

"Yes!" He was emphatic.

"Come what may?" She had to be sure.

"Yes!"

She leaned her forehead against the glass. "I don't want this to cause a fissure between us, Rupert. I-I love you."

His voice dropped to a whisper. "I love you, too. And I have total faith that you can uncover the truth."

Her stomach clenched. "Alright. Then I'm coming to the funeral. Can you find me a place to stay?"

"Really? You don't know how glad I am to hear that. I was afraid because of what I said before, you wouldn't come. Dodo, it's like losing an arm when you're not with me." It was not a particularly romantic sentiment, but it was what she needed to hear.

"The funeral is the fourteenth? Expect me midday on the thirteenth," she told him.

After swapping a lot of sweet nothings, they said goodbye and she leaned against the wall of the cabinet with relief. It was going to be alright.

She looked at her watch. Four o'clock. David would still be at work. She dialed his office in the City.

"Hello. Inviting me to your engagement party?" He made fake sniffing sounds.

"David, I'm back on the case."

"Really? What happened to change Sir Lancelot's mind?"

She grinned a wry smile and explained. "So, I need to know what you found out about Lady Florence."

"Oh, how the tables have turned! What do I get out of this?"

"David," she warned.

"I'm just joshing. The gossip is all the reward I need."

She heard an odd noise. "What's happening?"

"I'm getting comfortable. Your little Lady Florence Tingey has a lot of secrets for someone who is so closely related to the royal family."

"Are any of them relevant?" she asked, her spirits rising.

"How about this; Lady Florence was promised to Lord Falwell, who is fifteen years her senior, from the tender age of ten. But when it was time for the official engagement to be announced, she bolted to Europe."

"Where she met Rafe," finished Dodo. "But didn't mention anything about an arranged marriage to him." She tapped her lips, her mind working overtime. "What has become of that betrothal? Is it still in effect?"

"No, and not for the reason you think. She was sent to a French finishing school at sixteen and was expelled." His voice had become overly dramatic.

"For what, missing lights out?" she asked.

"Nothing so ordinary, darling. No! She ran away with the headmistress's son!" David was thoroughly enjoying himself, and Lady Florence's conduct was disgraceful.

"Ooh, là, là!"

"Indeed. They had got all the way to Belgium before they were found *two weeks later*."

"That *is* a scandal," Dodo agreed.

"Lord Falwell had no idea, but when she embarrassed him by running away from the engagement, he did some investigating of his own and got wind of it. He broke off their understanding on the strength of the sordidness of her sins, while she was still in Europe the second time around. He is now married to the Duke of Lethbridge's youngest daughter."

"So, the crime of running away with someone, without being married, caused small ripples in high society but was kept off of the front pages," mused Dodo tapping her nails.

"That is the benefit of having relatives in the highest of places," agreed David.

"So, what about the chap she broke Rafe's heart over. Who is he?"

"That is not as it seems either. His name is Lord Warwick. He is a marquess. As I heard it, Lady Florence has a bad habit of frequenting clubs with dangerous reputations. She's a mess really. That fellow, Warwick, is forcing her to keep company with him through blackmail. She's a pretty little thing and no mistaking, but she is not in a genuine relationship with him." David paused for dramatic effect. "My sources also tell me that when Rafe was embarrassed by her apparent infidelity, she pleaded with him to rescue her from Lord Warwick, but he refused."

"What is the state of things now?"

"Warwick must have something truly terrible to hang over her head because they are seen around London quite frequently."

Could Florence have been angry enough to confront Rafe over his abandonment? It was possible.

"David, you are a magician. I don't suppose you have any information about Max Fortnon or Captain Theodore Lindley?"

"Well, you called me off..." His comment ended on a high note.
"But?"

"I might have been curious about Mr. Fortnon."

"Thank heavens!" declared Dodo.

"He is actually one of the descendants of the original Fortnon and as such will inherit a tidy sum and estate from the chain of stores. Did you know that the earlier Fortnon rented a room in Martin's house in the early 1700s?"

"I did not," she replied.

"That was how the two met. Mr. Martin had a small food stall in St. James's Market and Mr. Fortnon was of an entrepreneurial temperament. They put their heads together to produce portable food. Thus, was born the Welsh Egg."

"And now it is an empire," murmured Dodo.

"Quite. Mr. Max Fortnon has been indulged his whole life and I couldn't find a single person who likes him."

"Being an unlikeable, rich man does not make one a murderer," she retorted.

"That is quite true, thankfully, but...it appears that Mr. Max is not above a little extortion. He started small at Eaton, graduated at Cambridge and has his fingers in quite a few schemes today."

"Did you find any crossover between him and Rafe?" she asked.

"I did not give the task my full effort, my dear, because you had dropped the investigation, but now that I have authority from you to continue, I'll look into it," he responded.

"You are a marvel."

"Tell me something I don't know, darling."

"Nothing on Captain Lindley?" She knew she was pushing her luck.

"He may prove more difficult since he is not part of the London scene, but I'll see what I can do."

"David, thank you." She made a kissing sound into the telephone.

"Think nothing of it. You'll just owe me."

Chapter 9

For a small, family chapel, the rib vaulting on the ceiling of the church on the Alleyn estate was masterful, and the stained-glass windows magnificent. However, the heady scent of the intricate flower arrangements flanking the altar was almost too overpowering in the small space. Majestic organ music drowned out the sobbing of Rafe's mother as she sat huddled like a cat caught in a storm, next to her sister.

Chairs had been brought in to accommodate the mourners but there were still people standing on the edges and an overflow past the double doors. When the young died there were plenty to mourn them. A subdued, haggard Hugh was out on bail and in attendance with Rosamund, at the end of Dodo's pew. Juliette and Jasper were between them and Rupert. The captain was in the front row with the family, in full dress uniform. Dodo craned her neck and caught a glimpse of Robert Dalrymple and Poppy Drinkwater near the back of the crowd.

A rustling from the rear indicated that it was time to rise, and the pall bearers brought in a mahogany casket draped in a Union Jack and more flowers. A general veil of grief hung over the entire congregation. Lady Alleyn was helped to her feet by her sister and the captain.

As Dodo and Rupert stepped out into the healing sunshine after the service, she caught sight of Inspector Bradford hanging around the trees on the periphery of the graveyard. He was squinting at all the congregants. She and Rupert followed the crowd to the burial plot where a gaping hole yawned next to the graves of Rafe's father and grandparents. Lady Alleyn wore a hat with a heavy veil which she kept pushing up to dab her face as she leaned against her sister.

Rupert reached for Dodo's hand. Eyes red and swollen, she sensed he was on the verge of an emotional breakdown as he stared into the six-foot hole. She traced, *I love you*, onto his palm with her finger.

As the vicar began the liturgy for the burial, Dodo looked around. Captain Lindley's jaw was clenched as tight as were his fists that hung at his sides. Hugh was a mess as Rosamund tried to comfort him by rubbing his arm. Juliette and Jasper appeared to be lost in a trance, their eyes open but not seeing.

A late arrival caught Dodo's attention. An exceptionally well-dressed woman stepped out of a black limousine and looked toward the group around the grave. She wore a highly stylish hat with a small veil that exposed small blonde curls. A husky man stepped out immediately after her, looking left and right then roughly taking her arm.

As the stoic, young woman drew closer, Dodo was impressed with her impeccable make-up and tiny features. Was she looking at Lady Florence Tingey? Pushing her way through the crowd and leaving her companion in the back, the newcomer stared at the suspended coffin, her features crumpling like paper in a flame. Rupert stared at the girl from across the plot then cast panicked eyes at Dodo.

As the graveside service ended, Lady Alleyn dropped soil onto her son's coffin, swiftly losing her ability to stand upright. Captain Lindley propped her up, throwing his own handful of soil then helping her to a waiting car.

"That was ruddy awful," said Jasper as he blew his nose with a wrinkled handkerchief. "Up until now I suppose I had hoped it was all a colossal mistake and that Rafe hadn't really died. Funerals are so...final."

"Are you going back to the house?" Rupert asked.

"Don't feel much like going, but I suppose we must pay our respects," Jasper said. "His poor mother looks done in. I don't think we'll stay long."

Hugh nodded toward the inspector. "I think he's here keeping an eye on me."

"Perhaps," said Dodo, "but it is a common practice for the police to attend the funeral of a victim. They hope to watch everyone concerned in the hopes of learning things."

"Well, it's bally intrusive," Hugh complained. "Grieving is a personal activity and knowing that the person who thinks you put your friend in the ground is hovering, makes it a hundred times worse."

"What evidence did they have that led to your arrest?" Dodo asked.

"That I went back into the stable area sometime after you and Rupert and the others left. I knew it would look bad, so I didn't mention it in my initial interview. It was nothing, but it was stupid not to mention it. A witness saw me. I finally admitted it to the inspector, but the thing is, I heard Rafe with someone in the changing room. They were still in a heated, low discussion when I left which should prove my innocence, but no other witness has confirmed the presence of another person in there with Rafe. But I swear to you, Rafe was talking to someone else when I left. Without corroboration, it makes me the last person to see him alive."

She thought of Juliette claiming to see someone wearing dark clothes running from the scene, but she could not give a description, and no one had come forward.

"What about the groom as a suspect?" she asked.

"The doctor puts Rafe's death at between six and four hours before the body was found which gives the groom an ironclad alibi. He was home with his wife helping his son learn to ride a bicycle. Me on the other hand, I admitted to being there within that window of time. And the press is anxious for an arrest."

"So, that's means and opportunity but what about your motive?" Dodo asked, watching the inspector return to his car.

Hugh dipped his head. "This is extremely embarrassing, and I am thoroughly ashamed about my behavior, but a week or so ago I suspected Rafe of having feelings for Rosamund."

Rosamund took a step back. "What?"

"It's jealousy mingled with a lack of confidence. I caught him looking at you in a way I didn't like—and at the time I had no idea

65

that you two had a past. I confronted him about it at a practice and he told me I was delusional and that he was still getting over Florence. He made me see sense, but someone who was saddling up their horse heard us and told the police."

This was an unexpected setback which placed Hugh right at the top of Dodo's own list of suspects. "It's obviously not enough, since they let you go, but I trust you have a good solicitor."

"The best money can buy. My father has complete trust in my innocence and will stop at nothing to clear my name."

And his own in the process.

Rosamund was studying Hugh as if he were a stranger and Dodo wondered if his temper would lead to a breaking of the engagement. Trust was the bedrock of a healthy relationship and Hugh's supply seemed bankrupt.

They all began the short walk to the manor house. Hugh and Rosamund were walking together but not touching, engaged in intense conversation.

"Has his temper been an issue before?" she whispered to Rupert and Jasper.

They glanced at each other. "It has," admitted Rupert. "But it's usually a storm in a teacup. And he masters it on the field, unless there's cheating or a bad call by the umpires. Then it leaks out."

"Well, I can totally comprehend why the inspector arrested him. We'll just have to find someone with an even more incriminating motive," she said. "And fancy Florence turning up!"

"Bad show that is," spat out Rupert. "Why do uninvited people push their way in to funerals? It is a complete invasion of privacy."

"Couldn't agree more," said Jasper. "She broke his heart and has the nerve to show up here. It's the height of insensitivity."

Dodo decided this was not the moment to reveal what David had discovered about the state of Florence's own heart.

"I'm only glad Rafe's mother was in the dark about the whole thing," Jasper continued.

"What do you mean?" asked Dodo.

"While Rafe and Florence were in Europe, she asked him not to mention their relationship to his family."

"Did she say why?" Dodo persisted, interested to see how much his friends already knew.

"Some story about an angry former love," said Jasper. "Isn't that about the tall and short of it, Rupert?"

"That's what Rafe told me," Rupert agreed.

They walked along in silence for a while, enjoying the warmth of the spring sun.

"What do you all know about Rafe's cousin, the stalwart captain?" asked Dodo as they approached the house and saw Theodore Lindley welcoming people.

"Not a lot," said Jasper. "I don't even know if he's the heir. Do you?" he asked Rupert.

"I don't, but the fact that he's with Rafe's mother now and acting as the host, leads me to conclude that he *is* the new earl. He must be the son of one of Rafe's uncles or something."

"I suppose we will find out soon enough," said Jasper.

"Welcome," said the captain. "Drinks and nibbles are in the main entrance."

Unlike her own home, the Alleyn's mansion did not have stone stairs up to the main entrance. Indeed, the ornate, front door was at ground level, surrounded by two arched windows. The central, front portion of the house was a Grecian type façade with mock pillars. This was in turn flanked by wings of local stone each with an upper balustrade parapet.

The entrance hall was a large room with black and white tiled floor and stone arches framing the entrances of two staircases that met at the top. The high, vaulted ceiling was lined with carved oak images. Several tables had been laden with delicate sandwiches, French cheeses and cakes. Large silver punch bowls were set on the end of each table.

A flash of fake platinum hair caught Dodo's eye and she gasped. *Veronica!* What was *she* doing here? She had not attended the funeral.

Without saying a word, Dodo tipped her head in Veronica's direction. For the second time, Rupert's eyes filled with panic.

"What the blazes?" he blurted out.

"She was at the game that day," said Dodo in disbelief. "She was cheering for someone on the other team. But I cannot fathom why she's here today."

Veronica had taken mourning clothes and made them into a spectacle containing far too many feathers. As they watched her tottering progress along the food tables in horror, Dodo gasped as she was joined by Florence Tingey. When the two women hugged and kissed each other with the stern lover in tow, Dodo could not hide her disdain.

"Well, that's a turn-up for the books. How on earth do they know each other?"

The large entrance hall was filling up with people and Dodo and Rupert moved to the edge of the square, clutching small china plates and glass punch cups. Rupert was not touching his food but Dodo was hungry after the emotional exhaustion of the funeral. She dragged her eyes from Veronica and Florence to search for Lady Alleyn. She sat in the corner in an armchair that had been brought in for the occasion. A ghost could not have looked more pale. She was the very picture of sorrow.

An all too familiar screech caused everyone to stop talking and search for the cause. The center of unwanted attention, Veronica put a hand over her face as an attempt at an insincere apology. As people tutted in disgust at her outburst, Veronica's sheepishness was at least evidence that she had the decency to appreciate that such irreverent behavior was ill suited to a funeral luncheon.

"I am terribly sorry," Veronica gushed to the room in general. "How silly of me."

The general hum of conversation began again, and Dodo watched in horrified fascination as Veronica left Florence and made her way toward the solid captain.

This should be entertaining.

However, the captain reached down and kissed Veronica on the cheek. *They know each other too!*

Dodo paid careful attention to the body language of both. Veronica draped herself on the banister, touching the captain's arm and giggling like a schoolgirl as the captain shuffled back slightly, a fixed smile on his face. *Hah!* She was not welcome. Only Veronica would try flirting at a funeral. Was she really aiming her Cupid's arrow at the new earl? That seemed entirely plausible.

The captain said something low to her and then stepped up a few stairs and tapped his crystal glass with a spoon.

"On behalf of the family, I would like to thank you all for coming to pay your respects to my cousin. Of course, the unfortunate circumstances of his departing does cast a pall of uncertainty over the occasion, but I have full faith that the constabulary will draw their investigation to a satisfactory conclusion and that justice will be served. You are most welcome to stay and share memories of my cousin but I beg you to excuse Lady Alleyn, who will now return to her quarters."

Captain Lindley brushed past Veronica and over to his aunt, gently guiding her down a private hallway.

Veronica spun on her heels and made a beeline for Dodo and Rupert.

"I knew you two would get along like a house on fire," she said, smoothing her white, Marcel waves and pulling out a cigarette holder. She dug in her clutch for a cigarette case and placing the item in the end of the holder, held it out for Rupert to light. She sucked in a huge breath and then let the white smoke spiral into Dodo's face. She coughed.

"I am surprised to see you here," said Rupert, putting the lighter back in his pocket.

"Well, I make the rounds of the polo and knew Rafe a little, but I'm friends with Florence who still held a candle for him." She glanced back at Lady Florence who was now back in the company of the man she had arrived with. "I couldn't let her come alone."

"She doesn't look alone to me," said Dodo.

"Well, that goon doesn't count. I'm actually surprised she managed to come." Veronica waved her cigarette holder in the direction of Lord Warwick and Dodo watched the smoke scatter.

"Yes, why *did* she come? She caused Rafe so much pain," said Rupert.

"I told you already. She still cared for him," announced Veronica.

Rupert stiffened. "She had a funny way of showing it."

Veronica swung her arm and the smoke created a halo that was heading straight for Dodo. She weaved out of its way. "Oh, that was all a misunderstanding. Rafe was too honorable for his own good. If he had let Florence explain before going into full chivalry mode, he would have learned that she's not in love with the thug. She's still upset about it all. That's why she wanted to come. To apologize, so to speak."

What did the marquess have on Florence?

"Who is he, anyway?" asked Rupert.

"Lord Warwick, Marquess of Somerset," sneered Veronica. "Formerly known as Gabriel Ellis."

"Ellis! He was at school with a cousin of mine," said Rupert. "Perfectly detestable chap, by all accounts. He terrorized the new boys and bullied everyone else, even the teachers."

"Well, he hasn't changed much," said Veronica.

This only rubber-stamped what David had already told Dodo.

"You know Rafe's cousin, the captain?" asked Dodo.

"Lindley? Oh, yes. We met at a house party in Leicester about six months ago. We had a little fling, but I decided he was too stiff for me."

I'll bet!

Searching the room for the captain, Veronica sighed, "I suppose he's the earl now."

So that *was* the real reason she was here as Dodo had suspected.

She couldn't resist a little pot stirring. "Does that make him a little less stiff?"

Veronica laughed that high pitched screech that was her trademark. "What is it Jane Austen says? A rich man must be in want of a wife."

"Something like that," Dodo muttered.

"I may have been too hasty in my judgment," Veronica opined. "Thought I'd give him another chance."

Dodo thought she had about as much chance of snagging the captain as a domestic kitten had of taking down a lion.

"Too bad about Rafe, though," Veronica continued. "He was a handsome chap *and* had a title. Such a waste."

That may be the understatement of the year.

"You were there that day," said Dodo. "When did you leave? Did you see anything odd?"

Veronica took a puff and narrowed her eyes as the smoke floated in the air around her. "I was. I saw you lot leave. We hung around for a while longer then headed over to the pub."

"Did you see Rafe after we left?" Dodo asked.

"Of course. That's why I was at the game at all, really. I went to speak to him in private in the stable area. I wanted to tell him that Florence was trapped but that she still loved him. Convince Rafe that he had got it all wrong."

"What time was that?" asked Rupert glancing at Dodo.

Veronica rolled her eyes in thought. "Not sure. About five."

"How did he react?" Dodo asked.

"Didn't believe me and in no uncertain terms told me to leave. Said he had just got over her and didn't want to open old wounds."

"Did you tell the police?" asked Dodo.

Veronica crossed her arms, positioning the cigarette holder straight up. "They didn't ask me."

"Would you tell them now?" Dodo dug deep for an ounce of meekness. "Please."

Veronica tilted her golden head. "Why?"

"Because our friend, Hugh, has already been arrested for his murder since there was no one to corroborate his statement that he heard Rafe talking to someone. But it was *you*!"

Chapter 10

After some coaxing, Veronica reluctantly agreed to call the inspector the next day, before heading back to the food tables to stalk her prey. Dodo found Juliette and pointed out Veronica. "Could that be the person you saw leaving the stables that day?"

Juliette observed Veronica. "It's hard to say. The person was bent over and wearing dark clothes. They had pulled something like a wrap or hood over their head and I was distracted by the fight the waitresses were having." She kept her eye on Veronica. "I couldn't swear it *wasn't* her."

Dodo cast her mind back to the outlandish outfit and ridiculous hat Veronica had worn to the polo game. It was definitely not black.

"Well, thanks anyway," said Dodo.

Veronica had her hand on the captain's arm. His brow was deeply furrowed, his frantic eyes searching for a means of escape.

Lady Florence and Lord Warwick had crossed over to Dodo's side of the entry and Dodo decided to take a shot at her.

"Lady Dorothea Dorchester. How do you do?" She held out a hand.

"Lady Florence Tingey. Very well, thank you." Her handsome features had hardly moved.

The noble ruffian croaked. "This is Lord Warwick," she said with as much enthusiasm as a pirate on the end of a plank.

As if a light had gone on, Florence suddenly snapped her head to Dodo. "Dorchester? Aren't you the one who wears the fashions for that French company? I've seen your picture in the society rags."

"That's me!" said Dodo. "And you are friends with Veronica Shufflebottom."

"Yes, why? Do you know her?" Florence's gaze floated to the far side of the entry in search of her friend.

"Our paths have crossed." Dodo took out her compact, pretending to check her lipstick. "How did you know Rafe?"

Lady Florence raised haunted eyes. "If you don't mind me asking, how did *you* know him? He never mentioned you."

"That's because I met him for the first time on the day of the polo game. My boyfriend, Rupert Danforth, was his teammate and best friend. I came to the funeral to support Rupert."

Unexpectedly, a single tear tracked down Florence's cheek. "He and I...we used to..." She glanced at her surly companion. "We used to be close."

"Used to be?" asked Dodo acting the innocent.

Florence dropped her voice. "I...I was a fool. Let's just leave it at that." She swiped the tear away with the back of her hand.

"I understand," said Dodo.

"I came to pay my respects," Florence volunteered. "To say goodbye."

"Has it helped?" Dodo asked.

"Not at all," she replied. "Now, if you will excuse me. I think it's time for me to leave."

The brutish dope who accompanied Florence turned his untraditional face toward her. Some people might have called him striking, but in Dodo's mind, the sharp angles made Lord Warwick look disturbingly harsh. Next to the slight, petite Florence Tingey, he looked positively neanderthal. He wrestled her arm into his, and they left through the front door. Dodo experienced a startling wave of sympathy for the woman.

Rupert approached, growling. "Find out anything useful?"

"You're not going to like this, but between what David found out and my conversation with her, I think Rafe may have been her one true love."

Rupert made a guttural sound.

"I know you are prejudiced by your affection for Rafe, but that girl is truly grieving. She may be more of a slave to circumstance than we give her credit for. The man she came with is holding something over her—using it as emotional blackmail. He doesn't care that she doesn't love him."

"Well, excuse me if I don't cry for her," Rupert retorted.

73

"Hugh has had too much to drink," said Rosamund, hurrying over to them. "I'm going to take him home before he makes a complete fool of himself. I've called for a taxi to take us to the train station."

"Be safe," said Rupert.

The crowd was thinning as more people began to leave but Dodo was desperate for a private word with the captain. "Let's give the new earl our condolences," she suggested.

Rupert searched the room for Captain Lindley and witnessing Veronica with her talons in the poor chap, he begged off.

"Do you mind if I go and talk to him?" Dodo asked.

"Be my guest," said Rupert. He headed toward Jasper and Juliette.

Dodo ripped a page from her notebook and scribbled a message. Finding a footman, she pressed the note into his hand and pointed to Veronica then watched as the footman went to tell Veronica there was a phone call for her.

Only when she was well out of the way did Dodo approach the new Earl of Kent.

"Captain, or should I say Lord Kent, I just wanted to offer my condolences."

Waves of relief were still wafting from him in the wake of Veronica's departure. "Oh, just call me Lindley or Theo." He held out an arm pointing down a hallway. "Certainly, would you mind if we chatted in the study?" He looked toward where Veronica had disappeared with concern.

"Of course." Dodo followed him as they passed down a hall in the opposite direction and entered a comfortable study with floor to ceiling bookcases covered in leather bound volumes. It reminded Dodo of her father's study and even held the same faint odor of cigars.

"Please sit. Do you mind if I have a whiskey?"

"Not at all." She dropped into a threadbare, wing-backed chair.

He held the decanter up. "Do you want one?"

"No, thank you."

Instead of sitting at the desk he took the other chair. "What a day! I'm wiped out!"

"I'm sure." She waited for him to begin the conversation.

"Funerals are hard enough, and I've been to a few, but when the cause of death is murder, it takes the stress to a whole new level."

Dodo nodded.

"Poor Lady Alleyn is a nervous wreck. I've arranged for the doctor to see her after everyone has left."

This was the opening Dodo had been looking for. "I suppose she is not just distraught about her only child's death but must be concerned about her own future."

Lindley's face burst open. "Her future? Oh, because I'm the new earl? She need have no fear on that score. There is a dower house on the other side of the lake. I shall install her there."

"I hate to be indelicate Captain, but at some point, you will marry and will have to consider the sensibilities of your wife. And what about your own mother?"

"Both my parents are deceased," he explained, "so that will not be a problem. And as for any future wife, I shall make it a condition of our marriage that Lady Alleyn shall have the use of the dower house until she passes away."

"That is very considerate." Dodo made a circle on the leather arm of the chair with her finger. "I don't suppose you have any prospects to fill the vacancy?"

"What? Oh, you mean that Shufflebottom woman, I suppose. She's like an octopus. She attached herself to me at a house party and would not be pried off. She is not my type at all—far too artificial, but she will not take no for an answer. You could have knocked me over with a feather when she turned up here today."

"She is a friend of Lady Florence Tingey," Dodo informed him.

"Who?"

"The tiny blonde who arrived late with the hulking fellow. She's the one who broke Rafe's heart."

Lindley swirled the amber liquid in his glass. "I wondered who she was. She steered well clear of me."

"She came to apologize to Rafe," Dodo explained.

Gesturing with the tumbler toward Dodo he remarked, "It's a bit late for that."

I couldn't agree more.

Chapter 11

W hen Dodo arrived back at Beresford House after the funeral, Sanderson presented her with a letter from Poppy Drinkwater. She asked to meet Percy privately at a small park near Dodo's home the following day.

Piqued with curiosity, Dodo arrived early and installed herself on an iron bench in the shade of a large oak tree. It was a pleasant day and the park was filled with mothers and nannies with their charges, floating paper boats on the pond and feeding the ducks.

Within minutes, Poppy arrived by taxi and Dodo waved. Poppy was wearing a distinctive, purple, drop waisted chiffon dress with a becoming cloche hat.

"Thank you so much for meeting me. How was the funeral?" Poppy asked.

"Surprising in some ways. Lady Florence, Rafe's former girlfriend, showed up, and a mutual acquaintance who happened to be at the polo that day, made an appearance to make a try for the new earl."

Poppy's eyebrows rose. "That seems a little premature."

"You would have to know the woman to see that it is her modus operandi."

Poppy clutched her handbag with some ferocity, and Dodo remained quiet to give her the opportunity to speak her mind.

"I'm sure you're wondering why I asked to meet you." She shifted on the bench. "Memories are fallible things, aren't they? Sometimes we see or hear something that means nothing at the time and then an event will bring back the innocuous memory, viewed in an entirely new light." She brushed her cheek. "Juliette is one of my closest friends and this is so difficult to say but given that poor Rafe was murdered, I have studied what I witnessed from every angle and feel compelled to tell someone. I'm not even sure of its relevance and would hate to do something that would jeopardize our friendship. Juliette mentioned that you are an investigator and so

77

before I go to the police, I thought I would get your opinion on the matter."

Now, Dodo was captivated. "You can be sure of my discretion."

Poppy looked out at the pond and all the little children. "I arrived at the restaurant early that night. I was excited to pair up with Rafe and see where the evening led. I got there about a quarter of an hour early and decided to use the ladies' room to check my make-up and calm my nerves. I could still feel the tickle of his whisper on my ear." She glanced at Dodo with a slight blush on her skin.

"There was a double door into the lavatories and as I was between doors, I heard a heated conversation on the other side and recognized Juliette's voice." She looked up with guilty eyes. "I confess, I eavesdropped. She and Jasper were discussing some money they owed. It must have been a substantial amount given the tone of their discussion. It seems they had bet on the outcome of the polo." She met Dodo's gaze. "They had bet *against* their own team."

This *was* unexpected.

Poppy continued. "I was shocked, of course, but someone pushed into the bathroom, which ended the conversation outside. I high tailed it back into a toilet stall so that I would not be discovered." She opened her bag. "When Rafe did not arrive for dinner, I was disappointed but Rupert said he was often late, so I pinned my hopes on the jazz club. Then the news about his murder turned everything upside down and I forgot the whole incident." She handed Dodo a newspaper clipping. "Yesterday morning, I read this in the paper and the whole conversation came flooding back with crystal clarity. I think it might be connected."

Dodo took the paper and read,

Scotland Yard Breaks Open National Sports Fixing Ring

Following twelve months of careful investigative work, Scotland Yard arrested gangster, Mel Morrison, who police believe was the mastermind behind a national sport's fixing ring that has fingers in every part of the country. Using undercover officers and police informants, the Yard has collected thousands of pages of evidence that many of the nation's most prestigious professional sports teams, and amateur teams, have been influenced by bets that have made some people millionaires and left others close to bankruptcy. It is alleged that Morrison maintained a band of brutes who would intimidate those who could not pay their debts. Many debtors are distinguished members of the upper classes who have never filed charges against Morrison, to save their reputations.

The ripple effect has yet to be appreciated as it brings into question the true ranking of all professional and amateur teams in the nation.

"And you believe that Jasper and Juliette are mixed up in this somehow?" Dodo asked Poppy.

"They were extremely anxious, and it seemed to be a very large quantity of money they owed since the team had *won* the game they were supposed to lose." She grabbed Dodo's hand. "Don't you see? If Jasper was trying to handicap the game so that they would lose and Rafe hit that winning goal unexpectedly, it could be the reason he was murdered."

Dodo's blood ran cold.

Gambling.

She looked down at the article again and read that Scotland Yard was encouraging anyone with information about the betting ring to contact them at a special number. They assured anonymity.

Pointing to the number, she said, "I would be lying if I didn't admit that this has upended all my previous theories about the murder. But look, you can make an anonymous statement that would get the ball rolling for an investigation into polo. I think that should do for now, but I must warn you that if I conclude, from my own investigating, that this is relevant to Rafe's death, I think you must be prepared to make a full statement to the police."

"I was worried you would say that," said Poppy as a mother duck and her babies waddled by. "My nerves are in such a stew that I couldn't eat breakfast. I can hardly bear the thought of snitching on my friends."

"Like I said," reiterated Dodo. "At this point, I believe making an anonymous report is sufficient. Then you will feel that you have

79

done something. I would like to make some follow-up inquiries before assuming this has anything to do with the murder. I'll contact you if I think the two events are connected. I would be happy to come with you if you need support. I have some contacts at Scotland Yard."

Poppy's expression lit up with hope. "Would you? The very idea terrifies me."

"Of course."

A trail of children followed the ducklings, bread in hand.

Poppy looked to the road where the taxi was still idling. "I thought I would feel better after getting this off my chest, but the pit in my stomach is yawning even bigger. What a mess this all is."

"You did the right thing to share your concerns," Dodo assured her.

Poppy held out a hand. "Thank you, Lady Dorothea. I'd better go and make that report."

As Poppy walked across the grass to the taxi, Dodo's spirits were taking a downward spiral. The size and scope of the betting circle and the timing of Rafe's death did not bode well.

And it might involve Rupert.

Chapter 12

Since the personal nature of the case had already messed with Rupert's head, Dodo was reluctant to address the possible link to the national gambling ring. She was positive that Rupert was not directly involved but she wasn't sure if he suspected anything or if this new revelation would wallop him like a cold artic blast.

She and Rupert had arranged a date to go punting, and she had arrived too early at the river rental shack which was a sure sign of her agitation. She clasped her father's paper under her arm. It would serve as a catalyst for an introduction to the topic. The original, huge headline had hit the wires while they were all at the funeral but surely by now, Rupert had seen it.

The day was fine, and she wore a simple lavender dress with a cotton cardigan and a straw hat to keep the sun off her face. And sensible shoes. Though she much preferred heeled footwear, the last thing she needed was to lose her balance getting in or out of the boat causing her to fall into the dirty river.

While practicing different openings in her head, she heard a familiar whistle and turned around with a smile. Striding toward her, Rupert wore a straw boater, white trousers and a 'v' neck tennis pullover. As usual, her heart danced a little jig at the sight of him. Without words he pulled her to him and kissed her thoroughly. She came up for breath, gasping.

"Hello, to you too!" she said with a smile she couldn't contain.

"You looked too delicious. I couldn't control myself," he admitted. "I hope I didn't compromise your reputation."

She bit her lip. "Would it be reckless to say, I didn't care?"

"Absolutely!"

He paid for the punt rental and grabbed a long pole, pulling one of the flat boats toward him and holding it steady. Taking her hand, he helped her in, then pushed away from the bank. The canopy of leaves provided broken shade that caused the sunlight to dapple on the water. She trailed her hand in the river and quickly pulled it out again. In spite of the sunshine, it was still icy cold.

Rupert expertly maneuvered his way through other punts, forming a gentle wake behind them.

"How are you?" she asked, supporting her back against the wooden bench. "You know, about everything?"

Rupert wrinkled his perfect nose. "Hugh called. His solicitor seems to be a competent fellow and has managed to secure one of the best barristers available, in the event that he is prosecuted."

"You don't think it was him?" she asked.

Rupert set his lips in a grim line. "I've known Hugh for years. There is no way he could do this."

The moment was ripe. She pulled out the paper from beneath her legs and held up the headline for him to see.

"I saw that this morning," he said. "Terrible. If the integrity of sports can be corrupted, I have to wonder what the world is coming to."

She replaced the newspaper under her. "Do you think it could have invaded polo?"

He pushed up his lips with disdain. "Posh! The Prince of Wales is a player, for goodness' sake!"

"You've never seen any evidence of game throwing?" she pushed.

"No!" He frowned. "Wait—what do you know?" He dug the pole in a little too harshly and the boat shuddered.

Dodo told him about her meeting with Poppy.

"No!" Rupert stopped planting his staff and the punt was carried on the current and into the bank.

He pushed the craft away from the river's edge then sat on the seat with the pole on his knees, forehead creased in contemplation. "I-I-wait!" He tipped his head back, fingers pressed to his lips. "When Rafe took that ball and whacked it through to win the game, I was elated. But when I looked over at Jasper in triumph, I thought I saw the vestiges of a scowl. He quickly transformed it to a yell of victory, and I didn't think anything more of it, but now…"

"Please don't be angry with me," she ventured. "But do you think Jasper would be capable of murder if he was furious enough about the outcome of the game?"

Rupert shook his head, removed the boater and ran a hand through his thick, blond hair. "Killing Rafe because he hit that ball through the posts wouldn't solve Jasper's money problems," he said after a few moments. "He would still owe someone else money."

Dodo put on her own thinking cap. "Do you suppose this gambling ring has 'watchers' at the games? What if Jasper was accosted by someone who was sent to collect money while he was in the stables or changing room. Remember Jasper *says* he returned to fetch his wallet. That could be a lie to cover up such a meeting. And what if Rafe got in the middle of it? Is that the type of thing Rafe would do?"

"Yes, but he's not an idiot. He wasn't exactly a surly chap," Rupert responded. "However, I can imagine a scenario where the muscle sent by the bookies threatened Jasper and Rafe witnessed it. The heavies might have killed Rafe to get rid of a witness and doing that in front of Jasper would send a loud and clear message for Jasper to clear his debts as soon as possible."

Rupert began to shake his head. "I see a problem. How could Jasper go to dinner as if nothing had happened, having just seen his friend beaten to death? There's no way he would be cold enough to celebrate, knowing full well his friend was laying beaten to death and was never going to show up?"

Dodo ducked to miss a low hanging branch. "Are you sure? Considering both he and Juliette were frightened to death about the size of the debt they owed, they were pretty good at pretending nothing was amiss."

Rupert rolled the pole in his hands. "We've got to the part I don't like—where we find out all our friend's dark secrets," said Rupert with a sigh. "I suppose we should mention this to the police."

Waving her hands as if swatting a fly Dodo said, "Poppy was going to leave an anonymous tip so that will launch a separate investigation into Jasper. But the police might connect the dots and swing the light of justice from Hugh to Jasper." She looked straight into his clear, blue eyes. "Are you brave enough to confront Jasper? Give him a chance to explain his side of the story? Defend himself against the charge of murder?"

Rupert groaned. "I don't know."

Dodo leaned forward and kissed the tip of his nose. "Let's put in somewhere and go for a drink before you decide."

David had called to let Dodo know he had gathered more information on the case and they made plans to meet him for dinner in town. Rupert was unusually quiet on the journey. She supposed he was still mulling the awful possibilities they had discussed on the river, and let him be.

The restaurant David had chosen was typical of him; rather avant-garde. It had dark windows with gold lettering and inside the chairs and tables were all tubular. Bizarre shaped lamps cast a dim glow. But the odor of food in the air was positively mouthwatering.

David was already there, sprawled over a chair like a dashing Victorian cape, smoothing his blond hair and checking his appearance in the back of a spoon. He wore a completely white suit and black patent shoes that shone in the lamplight.

"Dodo! Rupert!" he cried, standing and making a great production of his welcome. He had clearly missed his calling on the stage and more than one head swiveled to see what all the fuss was about.

A waiter whose oiled hair was parted down the middle and tucked behind his ears, came to get their drink order and David ordered a starter for them all. Rupert hardly reacted, a dark cloud still hanging over his patrician features.

"Darlings, what a horror!" David began once the waiter was out of earshot.

Dodo reached her hand across the table to comfort Rupert. "It is all very difficult. I hope you have some news that will move us forward."

David nodded. "This gambling ring has tainted everyone. But I'll let *you* be the judge of that. When it all came out in the papers, I took another look at this chap Max Fortnon." David swept a hand under his chin, a gold and diamond signet ring winking at them. "He's up to his neck in it."

This caught Rupert's attention. "I'm not surprised since we already know the gambling has reached its tentacles into polo."

"We discovered that Rupert's teammate Jasper is involved in it too," Dodo explained. "He is not a bookie but a punter."

David thumped the table. "Well, Max *is* an illegal bookmaker. Not much of a stretch from extortion to gambling and fixing games. He's a rotter through and through."

Dodo and Rupert stared at each other. "What if Rafe was involved and had been pressured to lose the game and Max killed him because he disobeyed orders?" suggested Dodo. "We know Rafe needed money for the estate."

Rupert's expression cheered as this theory of events vindicated his friends.

"There's more," David said as the waiter poured their wine and set a steaming pile of muscles in front of them. Dodo breathed in the scent as they waited for the waiter to walk away.

"Lady Florence is in the company of a man called the Earl of Warwick. It is alleged that he is a real piece of work."

"We know!" cried Dodo. "We met him at the funeral."

"*Did* you?" said David unperturbed. "Well, I bet you did *not* know that he was investigated for war crimes."

"No!" said Rupert and Dodo together.

"The fellow has no conscience at all. He was brought before a tribunal for"—David looked over his shoulder—"deflowering a young French woman."

"He wasn't convicted?" Rupert asked.

David quirked a brow. "His men were all witnesses for the defense and provided him with an alibi."

Rupert let out a breath. "No honor! Men like that give our forces a bad name."

Cracking open a shell with vigor, Dodo swallowed the moist treasure inside. "Fishy!" She grinned. "Do you know what it is he's holding over Lady Florence?"

David leaned forward. "It appears that the little lady bore a child when she was just sixteen."

"Woah!" said Rupert and Dodo in unison. David was full of thunderbolts tonight.

"The war was still raging so she was sent to Scotland instead of Europe. She lived with some farmers who had a connection with the family through a servant. It was all kept very quiet."

"How did *you* find out?" Dodo inquired.

"Depression leads to inebriation, and inebriation leads to loose lips. Florence herself let it slip one day after drinking too much while staying with her cousin. The cousin happens to be a friend of a friend. As a gentleman, I would never repeat this to anyone else, but you needed to know what hold this Warwick chap has over her and this is it." He dragged a finger across his lips and turned an imaginary key. "I doubt it has any bearing on this mess, but in case it does, I'm reporting it to you. And now I'm erasing it from my memory." He wiggled his fingers by his temple.

Dodo's mind was working overtime. Could this scandal have any bearing on Rafe's death? Rafe met Florence after the war as she was trying to escape the arranged marriage with Lord Falwell. Would Rafe have thrown her over if he had known about the child? Had they even got so far in their relationship that a future was being considered? Hadn't Rupert said it was a holiday fling?

She drummed her nails on the table, the food forgotten. The unknown was the baby's father. Was he somehow woven into this web? She would need to contact the Scottish vital record's office.

"I can see that I just dropped a bomb on you," said David, tucking into the pile of muscles. "But I do have more dirt if you can handle it."

"Go on," urged Dodo.

"Captain Theodore Lindley, legal heir to the Alleyn estate as second cousin once removed to Raphael Alleyn's father, has been an intimate in the Alleyn family since childhood. Rafe's father was even named as his godfather. The will was read the evening following the funeral and there were no surprises but," he paused, and Dodo felt her pulse kick up a notch. "Someone is contesting the legitimacy of his right to the estate."

Dodo blinked. "Do you know who?"

David rubbed his hands together, eyes shining like a cat who is about to feast on a mouse. "Another, more distant cousin, has claimed that the captain's real father was not the man Lindley considered to be his father, though it *is* his name on the birth certificate. Lindley's parents are both dead but local gossip had it that his mother became pregnant while her husband was on his return from an extended voyage to the West Indies. The ugly rumor was buried and considered irrelevant until it was evident that Lindley would lay claim to the title and estate."

"If his mother's husband is named on the birth certificate, I don't see how they can contend it," remarked Rupert.

"Perhaps," said David knocking back another muscle. "But the original birth certificate shows that Lindley was given a second middle name that was not in common use. It is the name of the man the cousin claims to be the natural father." David's mouth pulled to the side, eyebrow cocked as he waited for the news to distill.

Dodo snorted.

"Well, well. I don't know how it will play out in court, but it will certainly halt the transfer of the title and estate until it has been debated," said Rupert.

"Either way the captain has been blindsided," said David. "He had no hint of any of this and is now facing the reality that the man he considered to be his father, was not. Talk about having your world turned upside down!"

"That would pull the rug out," agreed Rupert.

"There's more," said David with a wicked glint. "The man the cousin claims is Lindley's real father, is still alive."

Chapter 13

After David's revelations, Dodo and Rupert had decided that a visit to the captain was in order. Their excuse was that on hearing of his legal troubles, they felt the need to offer their sympathies. They arranged to meet him in the garden of a village pub. The building was a quaint, thatched-roof, row of converted, white cottages with chairs and umbrellas outside in the garden. Dodo and Rupert ordered drinks at the bar and took them out on a tray to find Lindley.

The spring sun was out but a cool breeze fluttered the umbrellas and Dodo was glad she had opted for a jacket. The captain waved a hand and beckoned them over. It was the first time Dodo had seen him out of uniform and the tan, argyle sweater rendered him far more approachable. In addition, his chestnut hair was free of the heavy styling oil, allowing the wind to ruffle the waves.

"Rupert, Lady Dorothea, please sit. It is so good to see you."

Rupert pulled out a chair for Dodo. "Everything seemed so settled at the funeral and now it's all up in the air. You must be frazzled."

The captain shook his head in disbelief. "Losing Rafe was a big enough blow on its own. He was the closest of my cousins. But now this legal headache."

Dodo and Rupert had agreed it was best to appear ignorant of the terms of the challenge since the claim itself had been posted in the Times but the reason for it had not. Dodo wondered if he was aware of the financial condition of the estate yet.

"Words are inadequate. I can hardly fathom it," he continued.

"That this cousin is contesting you?" Dodo asked.

"No. It's not just that." He tipped his head back and rocked it from side to side. "We've kept it out of the papers for now but," he paused. "This cousin is claiming my mother had an affair while my father was away on business and that I am not a blood descendant of the Alleyn's at all."

"Oh, my goodness!" cried Dodo. "I see what you mean."

"I just cannot countenance it, and my poor mother is not here to defend her honor." He flipped the beer mat on the edge of the small table.

"Were you a close family?" asked Rupert.

The captain shrugged. "About normal I would say. My parents seemed to get along alright, and I went hunting and sailing with my father which was more than most boys can say. He was so proud of me when I advanced in rank to lieutenant and would have been bursting with pride to see me rise to the level of captain."

"You are awfully young," said Rupert. "I only made it to lieutenant, myself."

A slight coloring on Lindley's cheek showed the captain to be a modest man. "It was during the war—a battlefield promotion."

"Good for you!" said Rupert.

"My mother was a gentle soul and the very idea…" Lindley's tone was pained, as though it hurt to think of his mother in this way. "If it weren't for the title coming to me this rumor would never have been dusted off. It's bally awful."

"If it's not too indelicate to ask, what is the cousin claiming?" asked Dodo.

"He is accusing my mother of becoming pregnant while my father was still on the return journey from the West Indies where we have some land."

A gust threatened to flip off her hat and she secured it with her hand. "Wouldn't your birth certificate put those charges to rest?"

"Well, I was born eight months after my father's homecoming, but I was always told I was premature. However, my mother did receive a man at the house while my father was away."

"That hardly seems conclusive," commented Rupert.

"This is another poison arrow. I have a second middle name that I was not really aware of until this week. It is the Christian name of this friend."

"But if your mother was fond of this man in a friendly way, might she not have named you in his honor? It is a common enough practice," said Dodo.

Lindley rested his chin in his hand. "Mother never told me, and it was never used. I only saw it on my birth certificate when I signed up during the war, but I hardly paid it any attention."

"And it's unlikely she would be bold enough to name you after her lover," said Dodo. "It would only embolden the gossips."

"How can this be resolved? Do you know this man?" asked Rupert.

Lindley spun the beer mat between his fingers. "I do not. That my mother banished him from her life after my father's return seems suspicious to those who have so much to gain by my fall."

An aging barmaid pushing the hair out of her eyes, came out to collect empty glasses in a tub. Dodo handed hers over.

"Is this man still alive? Can he be interviewed?" asked Dodo.

"There's the rub," said the captain with a long face. "He *is* still alive, but I don't know if I want to meet him. It feels disloyal to my mother. Plus, if anyone discovered that I had visited him it would fuel the spurious claims. The press are already having a field day. Scandals sell more papers."

Dodo could certainly understand that line of thinking.

"I suppose the legal people will talk to him as they process the challenge. So you don't *need* to meet him," she declared.

"But now that I know, how can I not?" he said, fanning his fingers on the top of the table. "It will haunt me for the rest of my life if I don't and he is not a healthy man."

"It's a real conundrum," said Rupert. "Would you feel better if a friend could go with you?"

"I'd rather not air my dirty laundry to those who don't already know. So, if I go, I'll go alone." His comely face was set in grim lines.

"Another?" asked Rupert. The captain nodded and Rupert disappeared inside.

"How is Lady Alleyn?' asked Dodo. "I suppose she is technically a dowager now."

"She's taken Rafe's death very hard," he replied. "She spent so much time without him because he and his father did not get along. And now to be robbed of him in her old age sharpens the sting."

90

His words brought a thought to Dodo's mind. "Did *you* spend a lot of time at *Farrow's End* when you were a child?"

Rupert returned with two mugs almost overflowing, white froth clinging to the rim. He placed one in front of Lindley.

"Quite a lot, during summer holidays and such."

"Did you ever see the elder Alleyn beat Rafe?" She hoped she wasn't poking the bee's nest too hard.

"Yes! He was a mean man. I was terrified of him. Rafe and I both learned to stay well out of his way."

"Did he ever hit you?" asked Rupert, taking a sip, which left a beer mustache on his lip.

"There was one time he came close. Rafe and I were rough housing in a room we should not have been in. A china vase was broken by me as I pushed Rafe. He was so scared. We did not mention it, but of course the servants reported the damage, and we were summoned to the earl's study. He tore into us and was ready to cane me when Rafe spoke up and said I had nothing to do with it. He took the beating for me." The captain's eyes misted. "That is the foundation of our strong bond."

"Do you know how Rafe's father died?" asked Dodo wondering if this was a question too far.

Lindley paused, chewing his cheek. Dodo was sure he knew something and was wondering if he could trust them.

"I knew nothing about it," he said, after a while. "I was in Africa at the time." He took a large gulp of the beer. "After Rafe's funeral, as Lady Alleyn was succumbing to the sleeping draft the doctor had given her, she began talking gibberish. I sent the maid from the room in case she said anything embarrassing and it was passed all over the servant's hall.

"I held her hand as she drifted off and she seemed to think I was Rafe, and said, 'It was for the best you know.' Having no idea to what she referred I played along and replied, 'Of course, it was.' Then she squeezed her eyes shut and said, 'I couldn't stand to see him hurt you, my darling boy.' As you can imagine by this point, I was all ears.

91

"I asked to whom she was referring, and she sighed, 'Your father.' Then she seemed to drop off, but I needed to know more so I asked her what she meant. She roused at my question and whispered, 'Arsenic. Just a little at bedtime.'"

Arsenic! Dodo tried to control her features from showing shock and chanced a glance at Rupert. His wide eyes indicated he was failing. But a quick check of the captain showed he was staring at his mug, frowning, as he told the tale.

"I couldn't believe my ears!" He raised incredulous eyes and locked them with Dodo's. "Then she perked up a little and said, 'The doctor knew what he did to us. He signed the death certificate. Heart attack. I knew with him gone you would come back to me—and here you are.'" Lindley's face tightened. "You won't report this, will you? She has known nothing but misery."

Lindley had just tossed them a huge moral dilemma. The law would say that murder was murder, but Dodo's heart sympathized with the tortured woman. "If it appears to have any bearing on Rafe's death, then I fear it might come out," Dodo said. "But we certainly won't implicate her. A man as you describe would have many enemies."

Between what David had told them and this, Dodo was beginning to feel like her mind was going to burst.

"What about this sports fixing scandal?" she said, steering the conversation in another direction.

"I must admit I've been so caught up in my own dramas that I haven't given it much thought," Lindley responded.

"Would it surprise you to know that we suspect it infiltrated polo?"

"Really?" Lindley looked at Rupert.

"I didn't know anything about it, but we now have pretty solid evidence that we were supposed to lose that game on Saturday."

"Supposed to?" asked Lindley.

"Jasper was idiotic enough to get involved in the gambling. He was supposed to ensure we lost, even bet against us winning, and because we didn't, he owes some very bad people a lot of money."

92

The captain seemed to come out of a trance. "Could that be why Rafe was killed?"

"It's certainly a possibility," confirmed Rupert.

"However, at this point the police are still focusing their investigation on Hugh Cavendish," said Dodo. "He now admits to going back to the stable area *and* had an argument with Rafe a few days before his murder."

"Didn't he say he heard someone talking to Rafe?" asked the captain.

"Good memory. The police couldn't corroborate that, but I bumped into Veronica"—the captain winced—"and I discovered that it was she who Hugh overheard that day. She's friends with Lady Florence and had gone to persuade Rafe that she still cared for him."

"Well, that's good news for Hugh, isn't it?" asked Lindley.

"Only if Veronica goes to the police and tells them, but I'm not holding my breath. Her confession might lead them to poke around in her life and she wouldn't appreciate that. She has more than a few skeletons in her closet."

"This conversation has helped me realize there is at least one silver lining," said Lindley, swirling the beer around the bottom of his pint glass.

"What's that?" asked Rupert.

Lindley grinned. "Veronica won't find me as appealing if I'm not to get the title."

Chapter 14

S itting across a table, the all-important notebook between them, Dodo and Rupert were ready to brainstorm.

"We have a long list of suspects and a variety of motives," she said, flicking through the pages and tapping the pencil against her mouth.

"Perhaps it's time to get them in some sort of order to see if we can see any patterns or inconsistencies," suggested Rupert, his hands behind his head.

"Alright." Dodo turned to a fresh page.

Captain Lindley/Earl of Kent

"He seems to have the most to gain," said Rupert. "A title and an estate."

"But the estate is not flush," she reminded him.

"Unless Rafe actually divulged that information, the captain would not know. It is still a beautiful house with extensive grounds."

"I beg to differ. The house shows signs of wear that as a fairly frequent visitor, he would notice. But you are right about the land and title."

She wrote,

Means – the mallet

Motive – the title and estate

Opportunity – He admits to going back to the polo club to retrieve his gloves and was seen by Juliette Honeybourne.

"Drat! I wish we had thought to ask him about his gloves," she mused. "But it doesn't *feel* like him." She doodled by his name on the paper.

"Should I be worried?" asked Rupert with a grin.

She slapped his arm. "I just mean, he seems to be a personable man, especially for a soldier who has seen too much of the world at war. And even after all that, he seems ill equipped to deal with a woman of the Veronica type."

"It is unlike you to let personal feelings obscure the search for the truth," he said.

She wrinkled her nose. "I know! I'm not usually sentimental. His tale of woe has affected me, I suppose."

"Just remember to keep an open mind," warned Rupert. "Who's next?"

"It has to be Jasper," she stated, writing down his name. "He's on the hook for a lot of money because your team won the game and given the urgency of the whispered conversation Poppy overheard, he doesn't have the means to pay it."

"It still beggars belief that he would bet *against* our team. I've lost all respect for him, to be honest." Rupert was a man of principle and a person without scruples was a puzzle to him.

She wrote,

Motive – anger at Rafe for winning the game, debt
Opportunity – went back into the stable area to find his wallet. Could have used that as excuse to explain his presence there.

"We only have his word that his wallet was the reason he went back to the stable area," she pointed out. "And we should check his finances to see just how badly he needed to win that wager."

"And how do you propose we do that?" asked Rupert. "Even your winsome smile is not enough to unlock a bank manager's code of ethics."

"Perhaps we can offer to help Jasper navigate the raging waters. As we said, from Poppy's tip, the police know he's involved in the betting ring and that will soon lead them to suspect him of the murder. If he's innocent he might want our help to prove it."

Rupert fixed her with his baby blues. "What if it *is* him?"

"Then we will be duty bound to inform the police. Is that a price you are willing to pay?"

His mouth was set in a firm line. "Though I hate the thought of nailing someone in a coffin, justice for Rafe must be our top priority. Let the chips fall."

She squeezed his hand. "People make their own choices. You are not responsible if their bad behavior lands them in legal trouble."

She went back to the notebook. "Who's next? Hugh."

Dodo wrote, *Hugh Cavendish.*

Motive – Madly protective of Rosamund. Suspected Rafe of flirting with her. Led to argument days before the murder. Hot temper. Prone to violence.

Opportunity – admits to going back to stables and hearing Rafe in sharp conversation with someone. Possibly Veronica who went to convince Rafe that Florence still cared. Will she come forward?

"If Veronica doesn't confess that she was there soon, I will call the inspector anonymously myself. Hugh's life could hang on her testimony."

"Your voice would give you away immediately," he grinned.

"Then I shall have Lizzie make the call."

"Right! Who else?" he asked.

"Max Fortnon," she said as she wrote his name.

Motive – bookie for the illegal gambling ring, a cheat and extortioner. Would lose money on the outcome of the game.

Opportunity – did not leave the polo club until some time after our group. Could have sought out Rafe and killed him. Need witness.

"He's certainly vicious enough," remarked Rupert.

Dodo twirled the pencil between her fingers. "What about the women?"

"The doctor said it was probably a man who killed Rafe," Rupert reminded her.

"Actually, I seem to remember him adding that it could have been an extremely enraged woman," she responded. "The only woman who seems to fit that bill is Lady Florence. Could she have been infuriated that Rafe would not forgive her and save her from the clutches of Lord Warwick? She finds herself in a pretty hellish situation."

"Now that we know more of the messy details, that is a possibility," he agreed.

Dodo wrote Florence's name on the paper along with the motive.

Motive – anger, frustration, revenge for perceived abandonment

"What about opportunity? She wasn't seen by anyone at the club that day," Rupert pointed out.

"Juliette cannot be sure who it was she saw slinking away dressed in dark clothes with a hood pulled over their head. It could have been Florence. She would know he was playing polo that day by a quick look at the schedule in the Times."

"True." He threaded his fingers through hers. "Now that we have laid all that out, what is our next line of investigation?"

"I say we approach Jasper. He must be out of his wits with worry now that the gambling thing has blown wide open. We can exploit his state of mind to our advantage."

To their surprise, they found that Jasper was living in a splashy townhouse in Cadogan Square that Rupert had never seen. The wrought iron railings had been freshly painted and the windows sparkled in the sun. Rupert knocked on the impressive black door with the brass lion's head. An elderly servant answered the door in a livery that had once fit him nicely.

"May I help you?" His tone was just the right balance between ponderous and deferent.

"We are here to see Mr. Jasper Boynton." Rupert handed the servant his card. The butler bowed low, directed them to a drawing room and disappeared noiselessly.

Dodo looked around. Pastel pink, velvet curtains were skillfully drawn back with fussy, brass flower hooks and the furniture was upholstered in variations of pink and lavender taffeta, all evidence that this dwelling was the property of Jasper's mother.

The door burst open to reveal a haggard Jasper who strode toward Rupert and shook his hand with a violence verging on desperation.

"Rupert! Dodo! Any news?"

"Let's sit down, shall we?" suggested Rupert.

"That sounds ominous." Jasper laughed, like a man dancing on the edge of sanity. He dragged a trembling hand down bloodshot eyes.

"We know about the game fixing." Rupert let the direct sentence hang between them.

A range of emotions spanned Jasper's brow; denial, surprise, anger, humiliation, finally settling into resignation.

"How?"

Rupert hung his hands between his knees, leaning forward. "Does it really matter? How *could* you do it?"

Dodo was surprised how pained Rupert was, how much his tone smacked of utter disappointment at the betrayal.

Jasper's pain struck eyes filled with tears. "I know, I know! I've let everyone down. I can't tell you how hard these last few months have been. When you know you will inherit a fortune, it messes with your head. You cannot settle to anything and idle hands really are the devil's workshop. A friend invited me to an exclusive gambling club—underground, by invitation only. You know the sort of thing."

Rupert nodded and Dodo thought of Rupert's underground party business. The difference was, Rupert's activities were not illegal.

"I was flattered. I was at the table with the big rollers, Rupert, being treated like someone special." He stood and started to pace. "Vanity was my Achilles heel. They played on my lack of experience, and I was too proud to admit it. Looking back, I'm convinced they planted professional card sharps who prey on innocents like me. As you can imagine, after just a few weeks I was up to my ears in debt. Then my bally pride exploded like a madness. After a particularly bad night of losing big, I was dared to bet this very house. I did and I lost."

Grabbing his hair with frenzied fists, he cried, "What was I thinking? I don't even own the deed. This is *Mother's* house, passed onto her by *her* mother and on and on." He dragged an arm roughly across his cheek. "Then when I was at my lowest, someone whispered to me about the sports fixing scam. They heard I played polo and said they wanted to get a foothold there. I was stupid and bought into their lies, believing I could win enough to settle the debt and save Mother's house before she got wind of it." He looked up, pained eyes pleading with Rupert to understand. "It's easier to lose a match than win."

A faraway look in Rupert's eye made Dodo wonder if he was replaying last season's polo games in his head.

98

"The game was almost over, and I thought I was free and clear. Then Rafe shot that ball through the goal right before the last whistle, and it was like a ton weight on my chest. I could hardly breathe. It was all I could do not to yell out 'No!'"

Dodo recalled Rupert's words about Jasper's scowl.

"First game of the season," he continued. "We're all still getting warmed up. No problem. I placed a huge bet, Rupert." He chopped the air with his hands. "Huge! And, then we won." He dropped back into the chair, despondency written all over his face. "Now I'll lose this house *and* I have to come up with a load of cash." He smacked a book on a small table beside his chair. "I'm in hiding from their thugs."

"You must know the lid has blown off the whole thing," began Rupert. "You're as likely to be arrested for illegal betting as anything."

"Honestly, that's a better outcome than the other. I will be away from Mother's wrath, and the heavies. I've felt the end of their anger once before." He rubbed his knee.

"Did you take out your frustration on Rafe? Was it an accident?" asked Rupert real fear shining from his eyes.

Jasper's head snapped up. "No! How could you think such a thing? I'm in enough trouble without adding murder to my slate." He moaned. "I've actually been thinking about disappearing to South America."

"What about Juliette? Does she know?" asked Dodo.

Jasper's face crumpled and a half sob escaped. "She knows some of it but not about this house. Her family are land rich, so she won't get much of a dowry but if her mother finds out about any of it—if I'm arrested—it's over. You met Mrs. Honeybourne. She's an ice maiden." He put his head in his hands. "I would have to disappear without Juliette..."

Dodo watched his anguished face through the eyes of a detective. Lost souls in hell could not look more tormented. But was his genuine sorrow due to fear of his mother's wrath or guilt from killing Rafe?

Chapter 15

Over the course of the last few years, Dodo had become very familiar with Somerset House, the keeper of all the vital records of England and Wales. However, since she knew that they did not keep records for Scotland, she thought a phone call might be better than a visit in this instance.

"Hello, this is Lady Dorothea Dorchester. I am interested in a birth certificate that was registered in Scotland. I know you do not keep those records, but I am hoping you can steer me to the right people."

"I can give you the telephone number for the Scottish Records Office," said a cordial female voice, "but you might have better luck if you allow us to make the call—they can be suspicious of the general public. Do you have the names, dates, and locations?"

"That's the thing," responded Dodo. "I have a general idea of the date, no idea of the location, other than that the birth took place in Scotland. I do, however know the name of the mother." She gave the clerk what information she had.

"I can't promise anything, but I will look into it and give you a call back."

"I am most grateful," replied Dodo.

Instead of hanging up she stayed on the line which took her back to the exchange.

"Wexford police station, please."

"Please hold."

After several clicks and office staff, she finally got through to Inspector Bradford. "Hello, Inspector?"

"Lady Dorothea, how nice of you to call." His tone *could* be interpreted as sarcastic.

"I have a question and some things to report," she said, undeterred by his snarky attitude.

"Fire away."

"Has a woman named Veronica Shufflebottom come forward as a witness?"

He failed to stifle a laugh. "Shufflewhat?"

"Bottom. I thought she might not," said Dodo, sucking in her cheeks in exasperation. "She's a witness who corroborates Hugh's claim that he heard Rafe talking to someone in the stables. It was her. She had gone to see Rafe Alleyn on behalf of her friend, Lady Florence Tingey."

"Was the Shufflebottom woman the last person to see him alive?" His tone had become decidedly more formal.

"That, I could not tell you with any certainty, but it is helpful for Hugh Cavendish, is it not?"

"Could be. I'll call her in." She heard him murmur 'Shufflebottom' as he wrote.

"Have *you* made any progress in the case, Inspector?"

"It seems that this national gambling ring even had its claws in to polo, but you probably already knew that."

"I only recently learned of it, Inspector," she admitted. "Do you have your sights set on anyone in particular?"

"Are you familiar with Max Fortnon?" he asked. "He was on the opposing team and is heavily involved in the game fixing."

"I had never heard of or met the man before the day of the game, but Rupert said he's a nasty piece of work."

"That might be an understatement, m'lady. He seems to be one of the key players in the polo side of things and we are watching him closely. Obviously, that makes him a suspect in the murder and we have questioned him, but I need more concrete evidence for an arrest. The *Sweeney* are eager to hit him with racketeering and illegal gambling charges so there's a bit of a turf war. I don't suppose you have any information that might help me?"

"The *Sweeney*? I am not familiar with that term, Inspector?"

"Sorry! I forgot who I was talking to. It's Cockney rhyming slang for the *Flying Squad*."

"That title I am familiar with," she chuckled. "They are a small group of specialized officers who gather information on criminals without being restricted to one geographical area, are they not?"

"Spot on, m'lady."

"How does one arrive at *'Sweeney'* from that?" she asked, perplexed.

"*Flying Squad* rhymes with *Sweeney Todd.* You know the notorious killer? Over time the *Todd* was dropped leaving *Sweeney.*"

"Thank you for the lesson, Inspector. I will amaze Rupert with my newfound knowledge."

"Anyway, as I was saying, the *Sweeney* have been tasked with uncovering the gambling operation. If it intersects with this murder, I will lose the case."

"I *can* tell you that I heard Max Fortnon is one of the bookmakers for the ring and before joining this criminal enterprise, was not above extortion and cheating."

"Nasty piece of work, as I said. How did you hear that he was a bookie for the ring?" asked the inspector.

Could she avoid revealing her source? "Now that it's hit the papers, there are all sorts of rumors. You would have to verify it, of course."

"I hope they nail the rotter for the gambling, but that's not my jurisdiction. From where I'm standing, I have no witnesses that put him in the stables that afternoon or evening, and no physical evidence that ties him to the crime."

"What about that matchbook?"

"We haven't been able to find where it came from. You?"

"No, sorry."

"Max Fortnon does smoke, but I can't tie the matchbook to him," said Inspector Bradford.

Dodo's conscience was nudging her to tell the inspector about Jasper's involvement in the betting but since she had no evidence that he killed Rafe, which was the crime she was investigating, decided to let him discover that on his own. She soothed her guilt by telling herself it was only a matter of time before the *Sweeney* arrested Jasper. He *had* mentioned fleeing but he was so besotted with Juliette that Dodo didn't really fear he would follow through on the threat.

102

Instead, she asked, "Did you hear about the captain's claim on the estate being questioned?"

"I did not," he responded, his tone spiked with curiosity.

Dodo reported the bald facts of the matter, leaving out the salacious parts.

"Well, that's a blow, I'm sure," said the inspector as though he were chewing a pencil.

"At least he has an established career to fall back on, in the event the challenger succeeds," she said. "But I do fear for Rafe's mother, Lady Alleyn." She definitely was not going to disclose that the dowager may have poisoned her abusive husband. Testimony under the influence of a sleeping draft would not stand up to scrutiny in the courts and besides, the death certificate said it was a heart attack.

"I'd better have the earl back for more questioning. His motive is as strong as any. He could have killed his cousin to get the inheritance. This new spanner in the works might make him less careful."

"Tread carefully, Inspector. I for one do not believe he murdered his cousin."

"And what are your grounds for believing that?" barked the inspector.

"I'm afraid I have no proof, inspector, I just like the fellow, and his good fortune is not only threatened, it is at the expense of a beloved cousin. Besides, the estate is not financially sound."

"Did he know that before?" the inspector demanded.

"I would think he suspected it since he was a fairly frequent visitor and the tired old house is obviously in bad need of updating."

The blustery weather was unstable, and Rupert was busy for the day so Dodo decided to look through some fashion sketches that had recently arrived from France. As an official ambassador for the *House of Dubois,* Renée Dubois shared the sketches with Dodo for the upcoming season before final decisions were made. She valued Dodo's opinion and innate sense of style.

As Dodo studied the sketches it was evident that Renée was attempting to raise the hemlines of modern women. She chuckled. Her grandmother, though progressive in some ways, was still scandalized that women dared to show their ankles and was of the opinion that the knee was one of the body's least attractive features.

The colors were drifting away from pastels and becoming more bold, which was exciting, and the use of other textures like leather, sequins and decorative buttons gave the dresses more interest.

One design stopped Dodo in her tracks. It was a bathing dress that stopped midway down the thigh and showed the bottom of lace trimmed, frilly, black bloomers. She leaned back and held the sketch high. Were there many women whose figures were forgiving enough to wear such an outrageous outfit on a public beach?

The clearing of a throat caused her to drop the scandalous sketch.

"A telephone call for you, Lady Dorothea."

She twisted in the seat to see a hint of color on his mottled, flabby cheeks. He had not missed the sketch.

"Thank you, Sanderson. Did they say who was calling?"

"Someone from Somerset House, m'lady."

She picked up the fallen sketch, stuffed it into the middle of the pile, and followed Sanderson down the hall.

"Hello," she said, on picking up the telephone.

"Lady Dorothea Dorchester?"

"Speaking."

"I had some success with your request. Florence Tingey gave birth to a girl in 1915 near Inverness. The child's name was listed as Constance Morrow with a note that she was adopted at birth and renamed. That information is sealed."

"Was the father's Christian name listed?" Dodo held her breath.

"Edward Morrow."

Dodo scribbled it onto the pad that sat next to the telephone.

"You have been most helpful. Thank you."

After replacing the receiver, she tapped the pad with her pencil. Morrow. *Morrow?* Why did that name ring a bell?

Having discovered that her mother was taking a bath, she knocked on the bathroom door. "It's me. Dodo."

"Come in, darling," said her mother who was submerged to her neck with bubbles up to her ears.

"You look comfortable," said Dodo.

"Oh, my dearest! I can still remember horrible baths as a child in a nasty cast iron tub in the nursery. Nanny would stoke up the fire before we began but the water would go cold so quickly, and I was the youngest and had to wait my turn. It was always freezing by then. I hated it. You don't know how grateful I am for indoor plumbing."

"Well, you look very snug."

"And when it begins to cool off," she said with a girlish grin, "I can turn the tap with my toe and warm it up."

"Lovely." Dodo sat on the edge of the bathtub. "Can I ask you a question?"

"Of course!" Her mother's lovely face folded into a frown. "As long as it's not about your horrid hobby." Guinevere Dorchester did not do murder.

"No, no. Nothing like that. More like society gossip."

Her mother's eyes widened, and she took a sip from a cocktail glass that was on a tray spread across the bath. "I'm always up for that."

"Do you know anyone called Morrow?"

"Morrow," Lady Guinevere murmured. She splashed the bubbles and sent some flying onto Dodo's dress. "Lady Gwendoline Morrow had a son, Richard, who everyone called Dicky. He was about ten years younger than me but an unapologetic rascal. I think he took things too far because his mother packed him off right before war was declared. But of course, he had to come back and then he was called up. He was killed at the Somme…along with so many others."

"That's sad." Dodo turned on the hot tap. "What about the Tingeys?"

Her mother's eyes snapped up as she lay her head on the edge of the white porcelain tub, her blonde hair wrapped in a colorful turban. "That's the reason Dicky was sent away." Her beautiful aqua eyes narrowed. "You know more than you're telling me."

105

"I don't know much, but I met Florence Tingey at the funeral of Rupert's friend. She was in love with him, I think."

"Who, Rupert?"

"No. Raphael Alleyn. The man who was—died. They met a couple of years ago while holidaying in Europe and he fell head over heels. I think they both did. But when she returned to England, she seemed to stray and was seen around town, cozying up with some other man. It gutted poor Rafe, but he took the high road to save her from embarrassment and broke it off. I don't think he ever got over it."

"Heartbreaking," said her mother, pulling the turban down and around her ears.

"The really gloomy thing is, it appears that the man Florence was seen with is forcing her to be with him by holding something terrible over her head. I believe he knows something about her past that could ruin her life and is using it as a means of emotional blackmail. I think it might be the fact that she had to go away when she was young. If not for that, she would still be with Rafe. And now he's gone."

"So distressing!" Her mother tapped the glass with a finger shrouded in bubbles. "I think the Tingeys are related to the King. That's why her mother was so insistent she be sent away."

"Full marks, Mummy! That is why this awful man's threats are so effective. He's a marquess. Warwick."

"Aggh!" cried her mother. "Your father has had dealings with the Warwicks over horses. Unscrupulous people. They tried to sell your father a horse that had been beaten and was skittish. Fortunately, your father is an expert and could see what he was up against, right from the start. One expects more from the gentry, somehow." She took a long sip of her cocktail.

"I'll let you get back to your luxurious bath."

As Dodo descended the stairs she began to feel quite sorry for Lady Florence. A tragic history that had prevented her from being with her true love.

106

She returned to the drawing room and picked up the sketches. There was a distinctive ice blue evening gown fringed with ostrich feathers.

The throat clearing surprised her again. They really should put bells on Sanderson.

"It's Mr. Danforth, m'lady. On the telephone."

She squealed and gathered the sketches into a pile before flying from the room.

"Darling!" she said, as she lifted the receiver to her ear.

"Dodo, the groom from the club. He's dead."

Chapter 16

R upert's news came like a thunderclap. She dropped onto the telephone seat in confusion. "What?"

"The groom assigned to our horses at the club that day, Eddie Turnbull. He's been killed. The horses are brought by our own grooms, but they also assign an in-house groom. All the grooms were interviewed early on as they are the ones most frequently in the stables, and they were all cleared by the police. The club groom had an alibi for the time of Rafe's murder, but he was reported missing by his wife yesterday. A search was conducted, and he was found in a barrel in the stables."

"You know what this means?" she asked.

"Yes. He witnessed something and became a threat to the murderer."

Putting a hand to her forehead she felt her energy sap. "How awful. Do they know how he was killed?"

"Strangled with a scarf. It was found with the body. I think this development rules out the ladies. They could not have lifted him into the barrel."

"I suppose you're right," mused Dodo, realizing that this shocking event narrowed the field of suspects significantly. "Do you think the widow would speak to us?"

The groom's cottage was in a little row on a country road. It was painted a happy, pale lemon while the one on the right was painted white and the one on the left, a pale pink. They all shared one long thatched roof.

Rupert had sent a message ahead to say that he wanted to come and offer his condolences as the groom had been so helpful the day of the polo game.

A girl of about seven opened the door to them and a younger boy, not more than four, stood behind his sister in the shadows. There was a pall of gloom over the residence as they stepped into a poky hall that held the faint smell of bacon.

"Follow me," said the girl, limping along the hall.

She led them into a tiny parlor. Rupert could have easily touched the walls and the ceiling. A shrunken woman sat in a well-worn chair by an empty fire. Dodo and Rupert claimed a small sofa in brown, damask.

The new widow raised haunted eyes, and Dodo was shocked to see that she was in her late twenties. But for the mourning, she would be a beauty. The children stood wide eyed by the open door.

A distinct line formed above the bridge of the widow's nose. "Who are you, again?"

Rupert explained.

"Oh." She nodded but not with real comprehension.

Dodo sent a discreet shrug across the room to Rupert.

"We just wanted to offer our condolences."

The groom's wife nodded, eyes shining.

"He was a thoroughly knowledgeable and helpful chap. I can't understand…" Rupert looked at the children.

"Susie, take your brother and go fetch some tea."

When they were gone, Mrs. Turnbull said in a mournful tone. "I told him to leave well enough alone."

Dodo cast a sharp side eye to Rupert. They waited.

"He should have left it where it was and tipped off the police," she continued.

Bingo! The hair on the back of Dodo's neck rose.

"Left what?" asked Dodo as gently as she could.

"The tie pin." She glanced up, willing them to understand.

A clue? Excitement began to dance on Dodo's nerves. This was more than she could have hoped for. She flashed eager eyes up at Rupert whose expression matched her own.

"I'm sorry. Could you explain? We know nothing about a tie pin." said Dodo, trying to keep the enthusiasm out of her tone.

Mrs. Turnbull wiped her eyes with a handkerchief. "'Course, you don't. Silly me." She pulled the handkerchief tight between her fingers. "Eddie was mucking out the hay a few days after the killing

109

of that young man, and he found a gold tie pin. He didn't think much of it since he's always finding things on the floor of the stables. He put it in a drawer in our bedroom and forgot all about it. But a few days ago, he came home full of energy. He'd seen a similar tie pin on someone else and asked them where it was from. He must have made a connection because he told me that he saw a way to get his hands on some money."

Rupert quirked a brow at Dodo.

"Our Susie needs a special surgery to correct her foot," the young widow explained. "We didn't have the funds, but Eddie went on and on about how he might be able to get them. I didn't understand, but he told me not to worry." Her lips trembled. "That was the last time I saw him."

"I don't suppose you still have the pin?" Dodo asked, hardly daring to contemplate the possibility.

Mrs. Turnbull slipped a hand into the pocket of her wrinkled apron and opened her palm. A gold bar with the Greek symbol for omega, sat in it.

Rupert took the pin from her hand, examined it closely then lifted a shoulder indicating that it meant nothing to him.

"And he saw someone wearing this at the club the day of the murder?" Rupert asked, keeping his questioning glance on Dodo. She shook her head almost imperceptibly. Dodo didn't recognize the symbol either.

"Yes. I told him to let sleeping dogs lie," lamented the widow crying freely now.

"How much do you need for your daughter's surgery?" asked Rupert out of the blue. It seemed a rather personal question to Dodo.

The grieving woman shook her head. "It doesn't matter. She can't get the surgery now, poor love."

"But if she could?" he persisted.

"£50." She wiped her cheek.

"We are so terribly sorry about your husband. Would you allow me to look into his death?" asked Dodo.

The woman raised bloodshot eyes. "Look into it? Are you with the police?"

"No, but I've helped them before. I would be honored to do some investigating for you, though I can't guarantee anything."

Mrs. Turnbull's young face dropped into lines of worry. "I can't pay you anything."

Dodo raised her palms. "Oh, heavens! I wouldn't charge you a penny."

"*How* did you know Eddie?" she asked for the third time, looking at Rupert, her face a study in tragic confusion.

"I'm one of the polo players that your husband helped. My close friend is the rider who was killed."

"Ah." She moved the handkerchief around between her fingers and turned to Dodo. "Alright then. I *would* like to know what happened and who knows if the police will ever find out?" She blew her nose.

"Can we keep it?" asked Dodo, as Rupert held the pin between his thumb and forefinger. "For our investigation."

"I don't know..." Mrs. Turnbull began.

"We'll take very good care of it and return it at the end of the case," she assured her.

The widow's lips twisted. "You seem like honest people."

Rupert handed the piece of jewelry to Dodo and she placed it in her clutch.

As they closed the little front door that opened right onto the pavement, Dodo withdrew the pin. "You don't recognize it, then?"

"Well, I know it's omega, a letter in the Greek alphabet," he responded.

"Which means 'great'," she finished.

"Not exactly an exclusive emblem, by any means," Rupert observed.

"Well, it's a concrete lead, at least, and that's better than nothing."

They bought a paper and looked for details of the groom's murder. It was a small story on page two; the national gambling business still dominating the front page.

Edward Turnbull, groom at the prestigious Hounslea Polo Club, was discovered deceased, after having been reported missing by his wife. Strangled and stuffed in a barrel, he was found with several large pound notes on his person. Police suspect his death may be linked to the murder of Raphael Alleyn, the former Lord Kent, who was murdered weeks earlier at the same club. The killer in both cases is still at large.

Anyone with information is invited to call the police at Surrey 773.

"Did you know he had all that money on him?" she asked Rupert.

"No. One of my grooms told me about the grisly discovery, but he didn't mention that. Makes sense. He needed cash for his daughter and didn't reckon on such a dangerous opponent."

"I think I'd like to go back to the scene of the crime," Dodo said.

No one would suspect that two murders had happened at the polo club, as business continued as usual. A sign revealed that a polo game was scheduled for that afternoon and the tea tent was being resurrected for the event.

"Let's start at the beginning," said Dodo. "Well, the *end* of the game. The stables."

The stalls were empty but filled with fresh hay in anticipation of the incoming horses.

"I assume all the players came back to the stables and handed off their horses to the grooms. Who else was in here?" she asked.

"Jack, my man, Eddie Turnbull and several grooms who came with the other players. The personal grooms remove all the gear from the horses, feed them, rub them with a brush and let them cool down."

"And which stalls did your horses go into?"

Rupert pointed to the second and third stalls on the left. "I brought two horses and alternated them. I think Hugh and Jasper each brought three, and Rafe just two, also. Then there were all the horses of the opposing team. It was pretty crowded in here."

"Do you remember where Eddie stood?"

112

"Have you been to Charing Cross at rush hour? Add horses and that's how it was. And we were cheering and shouting, and the opposition was calling us names. We rewarded the horses with apples and sugar cubes. I remember giving the mares their treat hurriedly then rushing to the changing rooms next door."

"Shut your eyes. Play it back in your mind," she encouraged him.

Rupert did as she bid, small wrinkles punctuating his smooth brow. "Hugh's horses were stalled next to mine. Jasper's were near the back on the other side and Rafe's were this side of Jasper's but further back than mine.

"Who decides where each horse goes?"

"The club groom, Eddie. He's told how many horses will be attending and their names, and he writes the horse's name on a board in chalk and hangs it on the door."

"The farther you go back, the darker it is," she observed as she peered into the depths of the building.

"Most of the light is from the open door but there are small windows up high. You will remember from coming back the night of the murder that there are weak light bulbs all down the center," explained Rupert.

"Could you see any interactions between the opposing team and Rafe?"

Rupert closed his eyes again. "Not specifically. I was eager to come and see you. But I do remember telling Rafe I was going to get changed while he was still fussing with his animals. He said he would be there in a minute. He could have had some kind of interaction then. I recall that I was almost dressed by the time he came in and we did a play by play while I waited."

Together, Dodo and Rupert walked to the building next to the stable where the players changed and kept their personal belongings. The two buildings were set at right angles. Entering the changing area, one could see clearly into the stables, if the doors were left open.

"Is the stable door usually open during game time?" she asked.

"Yes. It's really only secured at night," said Rupert.

The changing room was painted white with rows of wooden benches. Hooks were set at eye level above the benches, and wire cubbies for shoes were underneath. Narrow, metal lockers were lined against the wall for keeping valuables safe.

"How are the lockers assigned?"

"First come, first served," Rupert replied. "The combination is written inside the locker, so you need to remember it."

"Where did you get changed?" Rupert took her to the second row about halfway down.

"Rafe was another couple of rows over and Jasper and Hugh were in the first row, right next to each other."

"And the opposition?"

"They were all grouped in the back, in the corner on the right."

Dodo walked along the rows. A kind of thick, decorative wire was used to separate them. She looked through to see if she could see Rupert who was still in the second row. Even with no clothes hanging on the hooks, visibility around the room wasn't great.

"We know Veronica followed Rafe in here after tea to let him know Florence still cared."

"That woman has no scruples," huffed Rupert. "It's strictly off limits for a woman to come in here, for obvious reasons."

"Are you really surprised?" Dodo asked with a grin. "Now, how do you think Rafe would have reacted to Veronica's news?"

"He was still in love with Florence. Anyone could see that. Love is not a switch that can be flipped. I think it would have made him extremely vulnerable and confused."

"So, are you saying he was probably in a state that made him less aware of his surroundings than usual?"

"I should think so," Rupert confirmed.

"We also know that he went back to the stables to check on his injured horse because he told you that. Between concern for his horse and feeling unsettled by Veronica's disclosure, he entered the stables rattled.

"His horses were far from the main door and it was kind of dark by then. In that emotional state he might not have even noticed someone approaching him from behind with a raised mallet."

114

"That is a fair assessment," Rupert agreed. "And the stable would have been empty of people by that time."

They returned to the stables and walked down to where Rafe's horses had been stalled. It was much darker than where Rupert's horses had been.

"Stand by the stall door as if you were talking to Rafe's mare," she said to Rupert.

He turned and pretended to take hold of a horse's reins and stroke its nose, head down.

Dodo went to the back of the stable and hid in the shadows then crept forward, hands raised as if holding a mallet. She inched up behind Rupert.

"Whack!" she cried. "Did you see me?"

"No. It was too dark, and you were very quiet. If Rafe's mind and heart were full of the revelation that Florence still cared, and concern for his horse, it is quite possible someone could have struck from behind without him noticing at all."

"He was a sitting duck," stated Dodo. "Let's try it from the other direction. Pretend to pet the horse again."

Dodo hurried to the open door, then tried to slink in unnoticed.

"Your body interrupts the rays of light from the door," Rupert said, almost immediately.

"So now we know something we didn't know before," declared Dodo.

Rupert leaned against the stall door. "The murderer was waiting for Rafe in the back of the stable."

"Exactly! The murderer knew Rafe well enough to know that he would come back to check on his horse."

Chapter 17

Like a shapely bride waiting for the organ to begin, the white canvas tea tent was all the way up, staff bustling around like bees. Tables were being arranged much the same way they had been the day of the murder. Dodo and Rupert found the spot the group had occupied on that day and looked around.

"Where was Max Fortnon sitting?" she asked.

Rupert pointed to the back, right corner of the tent—the opposite side from where she had waited for Rupert.

"Good. I didn't notice where he was sitting but I do know he did not leave before us. Sitting here with the group, I had an excellent sight line to the door."

"We're not open till later," said a curly-haired, young waitress approaching them in a black and white uniform.

"I know. We were here the day of the murder and are trying to figure out a few things," Dodo explained.

The girl's perky face took a dive. "Gives me the creeps. When Mr. Granger told me there was another game today, I kind of didn't want to come to work." She looked up at Dodo through her hair and dropped her voice to a stage whisper. "He spoke to me that day."

"Who? Lord Alleyn? The man who was killed?" Dodo asked.

"Yeah. He told me I looked pretty and gave me a big tip to let him have some extra sugar to give to his horse. He was a very handsome man." She blinked quickly.

A memory was triggered in Dodo's mind and she asked, "Did you see the argument that happened between two of the waitresses that day?"

The girl colored and dipped her chin. "That was me and Margie. I feel awful about it now that he's dead. It was so stupid."

"What was the argument about, if you don't mind me asking?" said Dodo amidst the clatter of china and cutlery.

116

"The attentions from Lord Alleyn went to my head a bit and I boasted about it. Then Margie says, 'You think you're so special, well, he said the same to me!' I called her a jealous liar, but she showed me the money he had given her. I accused her of some terrible things but she denied them and said Lord Alleyn was an honorable man and that I should take my mind out of the gutter." She swiped her nose with the back of her hand. "Well, that made me even more angry and I demanded she tell me why he had given her the money if nothing had happened and she said, 'Because I saw him give his horse something earlier in the day'."

"What?" interrupted Rupert.

"Margie loves horses, that's why she works here even though the pay is better down the pub. She likes to go and pat their noses. Anyway, she went to see them, like usual, before our shift started and Lord Alleyn was there." She dropped her voice even lower. "And he was giving his horse an *injection*."

"Is Margie here?" Rupert asked over the racket of chairs being set up, his face a dull shade of gray.

The girl looked around and shouted, "Margie. Over 'ere."

A buxom, pretty redhead nodded and began to walk over. They had clearly patched up their differences.

"This gentleman wants to know what you saw in the stables the day that earl was murdered."

Margie was assessing Rupert with a practiced eye. "You were playing that day too, weren't you? I remember."

"Yes. Lord Alleyn was a close friend of mine," Rupert replied.

Pursing her lips, Margie ran a hand down her curvy hip, making Dodo inwardly cringe.

"I often go and talk to the horses before the game," Margie began, confirming what the first waitress had said. "Sometimes I'll take them an apple or a carrot. I thought the stable was empty and walked right in and down the center, looking at all the lovely animals. One of the stable doors was open and I was worried about the horse getting out, but when I entered the stall, Lord Alleyn was pushing something into his mare. He looked up all embarrassed— his face was bright red. I said, 'Oh excuse me, sir.' But I couldn't

117

take my eyes off the needle. He pulled it out quick and stuck it in his pocket. I turned to go and he said, 'Wait!'.

"He asked my name and said that he had never seen such pretty hair. He explained that he was just giving his horse some pain medication because she had hurt her leg the day before. Then he said that other people might not understand, and could we keep it a secret between ourselves. He was an awfully nice gentleman and I said I would. Then he reached into his pocket and pushed some paper into my hand. When I looked, there were two pound notes. Two! Then we heard other people coming. He put a finger to his lips and I put one to mine and we shared a giggle. Then he left."

"Did you tell this to the police?" asked Dodo.

"Larks! No!" exclaimed Margie. "I'm a girl of my word. But you two aren't the police." She looked at Rupert with a cocky smile. "And you are one of his friends, so I don't mind telling you."

"And this is what you were fighting about that day?" Dodo asked the pair.

"Yeah," said the first girl. "It's not often a nob gives us the time of day. Made me feel right special. Told me mum all about it."

"Me too," agreed Margie. "Well, not the bit about the injection and the money."

"And you didn't tell the police any of this?" asked Rupert.

"We just said it was girl stuff, which is true, in a way."

"Thank you, girls," said Dodo by way of dismissal. Margie's gaze lingered on Rupert and Dodo had to hide an exasperated grimace.

"What do you think Rafe was doing?" she asked Rupert, who was still ashen.

He blew air between his teeth. "I can't say for sure, but I have a horrible feeling he was injecting his horse with dope."

They walked to the tent entrance to move out of the worker's way. "You don't believe his schtick about the pain medicine?" she asked.

Rupert tipped his head to the side. "Rafe would never ride an injured horse doctored up with pain medicine. But now that I know about the gambling ring and the state of his finances, I admit I'm thinking the worst. What if Rafe bet on us to win? He wouldn't know that Jasper had bet against us. It's not the sort of thing you admit to your teammates since it's highly illegal." He made a pyramid with his long fingers, resting them against his mouth. "If Rafe had bet a lot, he might earn enough to fix the roof of *Farrow's End*. He usually plays *Maribelle* the first and third quarters, but in that game, he switched the horses around, so he rode her last. I didn't think much of it at the time but now…Oh, Rafe, Rafe! What did you do?"

He kicked the ground, dislodging one of his gloves which fell. As Rupert bent to pick it up, Dodo snapped her fingers.

"I've thought of another question for those girls." She tottered over to where the two waitresses were setting out the cups and saucers, Rupert in her wake.

The girls looked up with expectation.

"One more thing. There was a man in military uniform in our party. Do you remember him?" Dodo asked.

"Ooh, yes," said Margie. "Very dashing and awfully polite. I think he was a captain or something."

"Do you remember seeing him come back into the tent after we all left? He could have been looking for gloves."

"Oh, yes! I saw him come back in," said Margie. "He was hard to miss, but he wasn't looking for no gloves. He went to speak to a man in the corner. I think he was another player."

Rupert briefly described Max Fortnon.

"Yes, that was him."

"Thank you." Rupert guided Dodo outside.

"Well, today has turned all my preconceptions upside down," he complained. "Rafe a cheat and his cousin dealing with a bookie who is elbow deep in the gambling ring. What is the world coming to?"

"It's like two enormous spiders have had a fight and their webs are tangled together," she declared.

119

Chapter 18

With this fresh, disheartening intelligence, Rupert said he wanted to go and search Rafe's London flat which he still used, in spite of having inherited the title and estate. The apartment was in Mayfair and was one level of a fabulous, white marble townhouse. They pulled up in front of it in Rupert's little green roadster.

Not having an actual key, Dodo pulled out her skeleton key kit and within a few moments they were inside. She had not had the set long but had spent hours practicing on all the locks in her home and although not as quick as the criminal classes, she had become quite adept.

A tidy foyer held an oak table with a dish for keys. A double door opened onto a spacious sitting room with tall, decorative plaster ceilings, large, leather couches, and tall windows draped in flowing net curtains. A large, central crystal chandelier anchored the room. It reminded Dodo of her mother's London apartment.

They followed the parquet flooring to the other end of the room where stood another set of double doors which led to a comfortable dining room. Beyond this, more doors revealed a decent size kitchen that was so pristine, Dodo suspected it was never used.

Meow

They locked eyes.

Dodo dropped to the floor. "Here kitty," she called. An achingly skinny, black cat slithered out from behind a chair. "You poor thing. You're starving." She picked up the featherweight animal, prominent ribs pressing against her hand.

"I found the bowls," said Rupert. "The water one is quite large, though it's dry now, and the food bowl is empty. This little fellow would have died if we hadn't come." He filled the water bowl at the sink and placed it on the floor and the malnourished cat wiggled for freedom. Dodo dropped to her haunches and the small animal bolted for the water dish, lapping so fiercely she worried it would vomit.

"Let's see if we can find some food," she suggested, pulling open cupboard doors. After rummaging through most of them, they finally found a small can of cat food. Dodo searched the drawers for a can opener.

"Don't put it all in," she told Rupert. "Its little tummy will have shrunk but its brain will tell it to eat as much as it can."

Rupert put a few spoonfuls in the bowl and the cat pounced.

"How terrible. Did you know Rafe had a cat?"

"No, but he loved animals."

Once they were satisfied that the cat was alright, they carried on through the flat and found a sparkling, modern bathroom replete with all the modern conveniences.

"I can almost smell the paint," said Dodo with a wink.

Rupert sighed. "I think we know where he got the money for this." If the Grim Reaper himself had stepped out of the gleaming tub, Rupert could not have looked more disappointed.

Moving on, they came to a large, masculine bedroom in dark blues and greens. A messy, canopy bed standing in the middle, took Dodo's breath away. Its disheveled state seemed to suggest that Rafe would burst through the door at any moment.

"Do you know how long the Alleyns have had this place?" she asked.

"Generations, I think. But it didn't look like this the last time I came here."

"I'll take the bathroom," she said, leaving Rupert to search the bedroom.

The whole thing was covered in gleaming, white tiles, edged with black. The oversized, chrome taps shone in the light of the stylish, silver light fixtures. Thick, red towels hung from racks and a crisp, white bathrobe graced a hook on the back of the door.

First, she tackled the mirrored medicine cabinet above the ceramic pedestal sink. Inside, were a razor, turtle shell comb, and expensive soap. Turning, she saw a small cabinet next to the bath. It revealed shoeshine and nail kits in neat, leather cases.

Empty handed, she headed back to the bedroom where Rupert was sitting on the edge of the bed looking despondently at something in his palm.

"What's wrong?" she asked.

He held up a small vial of clear liquid.

"Oh." She sat beside him on the bed. "Where did you find it?"

"One of the floorboards near the window squeaked when I walked on it. I pulled back the rug and using a penknife, managed to pry it up." He handed the vial to her. "It's a 'hopping' mixture made from cocaine and mercury. Supposed to give your horse an edge. I just can't believe Rafe would do this."

"From what Daddy says, it is quite common," she replied.

"Maybe in racing, but not in polo." He grabbed his shirt front. "The disappointment is crushing."

She laid a hand over his, "Well, the cost was high. Rafe may have paid for his poor choice with his life."

Discovery in hand they entered the charming Wexford police station, though today it was shrouded in rain. Rupert held an umbrella over Dodo and they stumbled through the door, Rupert flapping the umbrella to rid it of most of the moisture. Unlike her first visit, the waiting room was empty.

"Afternoon! Nasty weather!" said a desk sergeant they did not recognize in a lilting country accent. "How may I help you?"

Dodo explained who they were and that they had called ahead.

"Be right back!" He disappeared and materialized a few moments later.

"Inspector Bradford is waiting for you." He opened the door to let them through and Dodo knocked on Bradford's office.

"Come in!" His face looked strained as they entered. "You said on the phone you had something for me?"

Today the room was filled with tobacco fumes and the pipe was sitting in a ceramic holder, smoke curling from the pipe's chamber.

Wrinkling her nose, Dodo took the vial out of her clutch bag and placed it on his desk.

Bradford picked up the glass tube, examining it through squinted eyes. "Is this what they call 'hops'?"

"It is," said Rupert, and detailed all that the waitresses from the polo club had admitted to them.

The inspector sighed before picking up the pipe and resting it on his bottom teeth. "Where did you find it?"

Rupert told him about the loose floorboard.

The inspector shook his head. "Why don't the public trust us? If these silly girls had confessed this to us at the outset, my men would have known what they were looking for in his flat."

"They also missed Rafe's cat. The poor little thing was on death's door," commented Dodo.

"*That* is not my department," said the inspector wryly. "What are *you* going to do about it?"

"I shall call Lord Alleyn's mother and let her know," said Rupert. "Hopefully she will let me bring the poor thing to the estate—oh! That is, if Lady Alleyn is able to continue living at *Farrow's End*."

"About that," said Bradford, tapping the vial against a stack of papers.

"Has the challenger produced a legal document to support his claim?" asked Dodo.

"It will hit the wires tomorrow," said the inspector.

"An alternate birth certificate?" she asked. Hadn't the captain told her that his mother's husband, the man he considered to be his father, was listed as the father on the document?

"No, nothing like that, but equally damning. It's pictures. Some enterprising journalist engaged by the cousin, asked Mr..." He checked his notebook for the name. "Mr. Michael Russell–the man thought to be the real father of the captain, he asked Mr. Russel for a picture of himself as a young man. Lied about doing an article on old soldiers for the Sunday paper. It's uncanny. He and Lindley are dead ringers, apparently."

"What does that mean for his inheritance since his birth certificate lists the former earl?" asked Rupert.

"It means a pair of opposing solicitors are going to make a tidy sum battling it out in court," said the inspector, his hands behind his head.

"Will Lindley and Lady Alleyn be able to live there while the courts decide?" Rupert asked.

"No idea," replied the inspector. "Now, let's get back to this highly incriminating little bottle." He shook it. "Your friend appears to have been cheating and that leads me to suppose he was up to his neck in the gambling. That provides a plethora of motives. You start dealing with scumbags like that, and the value of your life drops dramatically. Those types will kill for the flimsiest of reasons." He wagged a finger at them. "It's starting to look like the former Lord Alleyn upset the wrong people and they took him out. Simple as that. And those gangs close ranks. We may never find his actual murderer."

The inspector grabbed the pipe out of his mouth. "I imagine the *Sweeney* will take over the investigation, now."

"What will that mean?" Dodo asked.

"I'm not sure, but once I file a report, someone will come and debrief me and take all my paperwork on the case."

"Any luck on finding out where that matchbook is from?" she asked.

"I've a constable calling every club in the London and Greater London area. He should be finished in about five years," he said with a sardonic grin.

"What about the murder of the groom?" asked Rupert. "Since it is presumably connected to Rafe's death."

The inspector grabbed his stubbly chin and pushed out his lips. "This second murder has us spread pretty thin and with the *Sweeney* likely taking over due to the gambling stuff, I am concentrating my efforts on Lord Alleyn's murder for the time being. If we can solve that one, the groom's murder will be connected. But we did question his widow. She wasn't a lot of help."

"Well, we went to pay our respects," admitted Dodo, "and we had more luck than you. She told us she thinks her husband was blackmailing someone."

The inspector sat up. "What? Blackmail! She never told *me* that. I could barely get a sensible word out of the poor woman."

"So, she didn't tell you their little girl needs an operation and Mr. Turnbull thought he could get the money through asking for hush money?"

"No! And that might have been helpful!" he blustered, holding his pipe aloft for emphasis. "To be honest, she wasn't in the frame of mind to tell us anything helpful."

Dodo's conscience bit her and she dug in her purse again, placing the gold tie pin on top of the pile of papers.

"What's this?" asked the inspector.

"The item Eddie Turnbull was using to blackmail someone," she explained. "We should have mentioned it earlier."

"You're a veritable Aladdin's cave of new clues," he mumbled while holding the pin to his eye. "Horseshoe?"

"It could be," began Dodo. "But it looks more like the Greek symbol for omega to us."

"Any idea what it means?" He nodded to Rupert. "Do you chaps wear these as part of your team uniform?"

"We do have a tie pin for formal dinners and such but it's round and has a flag on it."

"Hmm. How did Eddie Turnbull get this, and why did he think he could use it for blackmail?" asked the inspector.

"It was under some hay. He found it while cleaning out the stables and didn't recognize its significance at first, but then a patron came to the club wearing the same pin and he remembered someone wearing one the day of the murder. It's too bad *I* don't remember!" exclaimed Dodo. "But in my mind, the fact that Eddie has been killed over it, is proof that the murderer *did* lose it that day while committing the murder."

"Well, if you don't mind, I'll take this and add it to the evidence bin. It will all get taken to London by the *Sweeney* and maybe someone there will recognize it," Bradford mused. "Between that and the maroon scarf—"

"What?" Dodo interrupted him.

"I thought I mentioned it. Eddie Turnbull was strangled with a maroon and white scarf."

"No!" Dodo grabbed a piece of paper and the inspector offered her a pencil. She drew a diamond pattern. "Did it look like this?"

"Exactly," he responded. "You recognize it?"

"I do! Hugh was wearing one just like it the night we went to dinner."

Chapter 19

Rupert turned to her, hands up like he was surrendering. "That's right. He left it on the chair when he ran out of the restaurant, and I didn't remember to pick it up when we left."

"So, anyone could have taken it," said the inspector sounding more depressed by the minute. He rested his forehead in his hands. "There are so many dead ends in this case and people withholding information." Inspector Bradford lifted a careworn face. "Do you know, I don't think I'll mind having the Yard take over. To be honest, we're not used to murder cases here in Wexford and it has become increasingly clear that we don't have the experience or resources. I can hardly sleep for wondering about it all, and my daughter is about to have her third baby, any day. If I'm still in charge of this, I won't get to see the child before its second birthday."

"Well, we'll let you get back to it, then," said Dodo, sensing that they may have overstayed their welcome.

Bradford cast a suspicious eye on her handbag. "Are there any more clues in there before you leave?"

"Inspector Bradford, you make it sound like I have withheld evidence from you when, in fact, the very opposite is true. We came straight here from Rafe's flat."

The inspector grunted something as Rupert pushed Dodo out the door.

Back out in the incessant rain and under the damp umbrella, Dodo asked Rupert, "Do you think it is significant?"

"What? The scarf? Hugh was their main suspect at the beginning because he has a hot temper and was seen around the stables after we left, but I never thought he was capable of it. Most of the time he's a lot of hot air. And as the inspector pointed out, anyone could have taken the scarf because it became lost property at the restaurant. Besides, it's not an exclusive design. Other people own similar scarves."

"I'm not so sure. I'd like to call the restaurant and check if Hugh came back to get it." She took out her notebook and jotted down a note to call.

⌒

It had been a long day of running all over the countryside and Dodo just wanted to go home and put her feet up. When she and Rupert were settled in the small family drawing room, Rupert started massaging her feet and Dodo began idly doodling on a piece of paper. After several minutes her mother breezed in.

"Darlings! You're back! Has it been a splendid day?"

Knowing that her mother was just making conversation and would not really want to know what they had actually been doing since it was related to a murder, Dodo just smiled.

"What's that you're drawing? Oh, I haven't seen that sign for ages," Lady Guinevere commented as she fell into a large armchair.

"What sign?" asked Dodo her pulse elevating.

"That's the insignia of St. Helga's college for women, isn't it?"

Dodo held up the doodle. "Is it?"

"Not that way. That's upside down," said her mother.

Dodo turned the paper around.

"Yes, that's it. It is used in physics I believe, and St. Helga's college specializes in the sciences." Guinevere was already flicking through a society magazine.

"Mother!" Dodo shrieked. "How do you know that?"

"Do you remember my third cousin, Morgana? Protruding chin, large teeth?"

"Not really," said Dodo.

"Well, anyway, she attended the college in its inaugural year and never let anyone forget it. She wore that insignia everywhere. Bored us all to tears with it."

Dodo's excitement was about to blow out of her ears. "How did she wear the insignia?"

Her mother tipped her head back and closed her eyes. "It was a little gold pin worn on the collar. Looked like a tie pin."

Dodo leapt from the couch, smothered her mother in a bear hug and kissed her cheek.

"What is that for?" her mother said with a happy laugh.

"You clever thing, you have solved a puzzle!"

Of course, the knowledge itself was of no use on its own. She needed to connect the pin to someone, but it was a start.

Approaching *Farrows End* again, it seemed like months since she and Rupert had been there rather than mere days. After her mother's revelation the evening before, they had celebrated together with cake in the kitchen, but try as they might, they could not remember seeing anyone wearing that pin. Plus, the police had been adamant that a woman could not have placed Eddie Turnbull, the groom, into a barrel by themselves. Dodo tried not to let that dampen her enthusiasm.

Though the discovery of the meaning of the pin was exciting and visiting St. Helga's gave them a place to start, following up with Lindley about his interaction with Max Fortnon, seemed more pressing. An actual witness had given real testimony of a contradiction. Why had Lindley lied? Dodo suggested they arrive without announcement, declaring ignorance of the captain's current woes.

Sun rays shining through puffy, cumulus clouds, formed a spotlight, highlighting the white stone of the mansion house against the green of the meadows behind it. Postcard perfect.

"Is Lord Alleyn expecting you?" asked the butler over his nose, after ushering them into the grand foyer.

"Not exactly," admitted Rupert. They had timed their arrival to be an hour before lunch.

"His Lordship *is* home, however he is bogged down in legal work. His solicitor just this minute left."

"If the earl decides he cannot face us, we will gladly be on our way," said Dodo, which was a fib but one that suited the dour mood of the butler.

As they waited, Dodo looked around the large entry and replayed the ugly scene with Veronica on the stairs, and the anguish of Lady Florence, swaddled in a mantle of genuine mourning.

"His Lordship will see you," pronounced the butler and led them into an empty drawing room with faded Turkish rugs and mismatched, antique furniture.

"Good morning," said Lindley, bursting in with furious energy. "I'm afraid you have arrived at a difficult time."

"Oh?" said Dodo as innocently as she could.

He gestured for them to take a seat and they sat together on one of the low sofas. Dodo felt a spring bite into her and shifted closer to Rupert.

"You remember I told you about the challenge?"

They both nodded.

"Well, I went to see the chap. Nice enough fellow. His name is Michael Russell. He's in his early sixties now. I told him about the legal challenge and asked if there was any truth to the claim, but he said he would say nothing that would bring shame to my mother. I pleaded with him to put the matter to rest once and for all, but he refused. I studied his features and limbs for any similarities as he spoke about my mother during the time my father was away. In his present state, he is bald and carries extra weight and I could see no resemblance between he and myself. This was encouraging and I thought my visit had put the matter to rest.

"However, when we stood to shake hands, we were the same height almost to an inch. My father was not a tall man, but I am six foot four. So is this Russell chap." Lindley produced a mirthless laugh. "Hardly conclusive, what? So, I left, still pretty confident that the title and estate were mine." He pulled something from his inside jacket pocket and handed it to Dodo. "Yesterday, I received these in the second post."

Dodo took two photographs from him and expelled a short gasp. On the left was a sepia print of a young man in uniform who bore a striking resemblance to the current earl. Bradford had not been kidding. Though the shape of the chin differed slightly, and the man in the sepia print wore a bushy mustache, the general features were so similar as to be obviously people from the same family. In fact, it looked like Lindley, dressed for a costume party.

"You see the problem. Add that to the fact that my parents never bore another child and we are left with one conclusion," said Lindley with more than a little anxiety.

Rupert took the prints and studied them. "But without a legal birth certificate listing this man as your father, and without his admission, does your cousin have any legal legs to stand on?"

"That is the very thing I have been discussing with my solicitor this morning. He is of the opinion that without a birth certificate proving the contrary, my cousin has no case. However, there are worse things. This cousin, who I do not know, and who has no familial affection for my mother, has threatened to broadcast this salacious rumor and sully her character. She is not alive to defend herself. Indeed, he has already made good on his threat and we have had word this morning that a certain newspaper is going to print these in tomorrow's edition. They called to ask if I had any comment. I slammed the phone down." Color dotted Lindley's cheeks.

"I am so terribly sorry," said Dodo. "This cousin of yours must be truly despicable."

The earl ran a finger over his short mustache, showing the signet ring he wore on his little finger. "I think he was an ordinarily flawed person until he was informed that he had a slight claim to the land and title. If only he knew the state of it. He would probably run."

"Is it so bad?" asked Rupert.

"Since the funeral, I have met with accountants and the land manager. The leaks in the roof have led to a case of mold in the attics. In some places you can see right through to the sky. It will cost at least £1000 to repair it. We run on a skeleton staff as it is, but we will have to retrench. Every piece of furniture and rug in the house needs to be replaced. And don't even get me started on the plumbing! The fourth earl modernized during the late 1880s by fitting the house with pipes and primitive water heaters, but it hasn't been touched since then. A hungry dragon would make less noise than these pipes." He ran a frantic hand through his tidy hair leaving it in spikes. "The only choice we have is to sell off part of the land."

"Oh!" exclaimed Rupert as if he had been cut. "You have my condolences. The last thing a landowner wants to do is sell land."

"Indeed. I've hardly slept since I became the earl and part of me wants to just hand it over to the contestant. But I have more than myself to think about. Lady Alleyn is of a delicate constitution and the idea of her being thrown out of her home is intolerable. Furthermore, I owe the title to my future children. It is their destiny."

A solemn silence hung between them but the main reason they had come was to ask Lindley about speaking to Max Fortnon in the tea tent. Dodo looked for a way to introduce the subject.

"You certainly find yourself between the Devil and the deep blue sea," she sympathized. "Have you had any news from the inspector about Rafe?"

"And that's another thing hanging over my head. Who wants to acquire a title because their cousin was murdered? It's like a cloud of depression and sorrow is hanging over the whole house." He clasped his hands across his knees. "The inspector says they're still gathering evidence, which is a euphemism for they don't know beans, in my opinion."

"*We* have made some progress," said Dodo carefully. "It's a hobby of mine."

The captain looked up sharply. "What kind of progress?"

"Have you been following the news about the sports fixing ring?" she asked.

"Honestly, I don't have much energy for someone else's problems," he replied. "But since you suggested that it might be why Rafe was killed, I have read a bit about it."

Dodo studied him. Was this somber mood the reaction of someone who was up to his elbows in the scandal?

"Do you know a Max Fortnon?" asked Rupert.

Lindley frowned. "Should I?"

132

"He was a player on the other team, Heavy set, mean expression," Rupert explained.

Lindley's face fell even further. "The brute, you mean. Rafe told me this Max fellow gave him a hard time in the changing rooms. As only children, Rafe and I learned to stick together. I wasn't going to let this Max get away with bullying my cousin, so I did a U-turn back to the tea tent after you all left and had it out with him. Ah," he exclaimed as the penny dropped. "Someone told you I didn't go back for my gloves."

"One of the waitresses," said Dodo. "She saw you in a heavy conversation with Max. It has been discovered that Max Fortnon is one of the bookies for the gambling ring. So, you see how it looks. We had to check it out."

"Is he now?" responded Lindley. "Can't say I'm surprised. Horrid fellow. I just told him to leave Rafe alone or he'd have me to deal with. He laughed and said Rafe got no more than he deserved."

Rupert handed back the photos and after glancing at them, Lindley let the pictures drop to the coffee table.

"Yes, I see how that would look suspicious," Lindley continued. "But I swear to you, I had no idea about the gambling." He went stiff. "Do you think this Max may have killed Rafe?"

"I'm afraid at this point we are still sorting through the evidence," Dodo explained, hoping Lindley did not interpret the insipid comment as an indication that they actually knew very little.

Lindley sat up sharp. "Wait! You are saying that I am a suspect in my cousin's death?"

Dodo fashioned her features into her best smile. "We are merely following up on things that don't quite add up. When the waitress said you had a heated discussion with Max after you told us you went back to get your gloves—well, you can see why we became suspicious."

"I suppose so. But I assure you, I'm as eager to find out who did this to Rafe as anyone," he said. "And I can see it being this Max."

"He does seem a likely candidate, but we need proof that ties him to the murder scene," said Dodo.

She winked at Rupert.

"I suppose you own the London flat now," said Rupert.

"I suppose I do, but I haven't had a moment to think about it. Haven't been in years, in fact. I think Rafe took me just after the war. Right after his father had died and he was getting used to being the earl."

"In contrast to what you have told us about *Farrow's End*, the flat has beautiful plumbing. Don't you agree?" asked Dodo.

A startled look planted itself on the captain's features. "I don't know anything about that. It was pretty basic, as I recall."

"Then you need to go and take a look. That bathroom is state of the art. Gleaming ceramic and sparkling walls," she said.

Lindley shook his head in confusion. "Where on earth did Rafe get the money to update it?" His hooded eyes started. "Gambling."

Dodo couldn't help feeling sorry for the poor man. Could he take much more bad news? But it had to be done.

"I hate to tell you this when you are already dealing with so much, but we have good reason to believe Rafe was involved in the sports gambling." A thought popped into her head, but she kept it to herself.

"Just because he has a nice bathroom?" asked Lindley.

"No. Because we have uncovered evidence that he was doping his horses," said Rupert.

Lindley's face fell further. "Crossing those types of people would be dangerous."

"Yes, it would," said Dodo.

It was time to elevate the mood.

"I do have one more question," she said.

Lindley looked fearful. "Yes?"

"I wonder, what you are going to do with your new cat."

Chapter 20

Riding along in the open top, racing green roadster, Dodo relished the feel of the wind rushing past her cheeks. For a moment she thought about taking off her hat and feeling the breeze in her hair but thought better of it. The day was not over yet and she needed to stay presentable.

"I had a moment of enlightenment as we were talking to Lindley," she said. "Rafe *won* the game and was ecstatic. That proves his gambling is not connected with the large consortium because they wanted your team to *lose* the game."

"Brilliant deduction, Holmes." He reached a hand across and gently laid it against her neck.

Her heart lapped up his praise.

"So we need to find who Rafe was placing his bets with," he concluded.

"I'll add it to our ever-lengthening list."

"What do you think about Lindley?" asked Rupert, moving his hand to place it over hers as he changed gears.

"With regard to the title?" she asked.

"About his reason for going back to the tea tent. It means he was still on site when we all left. He *could* have hung around for Rafe."

"His excuse is plausible. You said yourself that Max is a bully and I can see that two cousins who are only children might act more like brothers. What do you think?"

"I still believe he may have wanted the title and had no idea of the financial problems that came with it."

"Wouldn't he?' she contradicted. "Even as an adult he must have visited *Farrow's End* from time to time. One can't help noticing the shoddy condition of the house and furniture. Frankly, you have to be blind not to spot it, and unless Rafe's father was a known skinflint, you would have to put two and two together."

Rupert shifted gears as they rounded a corner and the low rumble of the powerful engine passed through her body. "Hmm, that's true.

The carpets are threadbare and the sofas lumpy." He picked up her hand and kissed her knuckles. "Alright, you've convinced me."

"The publication of those photographs could be devastating, though. And how awful to think your mother was unfaithful, without being able to hear her side of the story. I personally feel extremely sorry for the poor fellow."

They broke through the trees into open land, the sun warming her face.

"I do think he'll win the legal case though," remarked Rupert. "If the old man stays quiet, they'll have to rely on the birth certificate."

"Do you look like any of your ancestors?" she asked.

"There's a cousin on my mother's side a couple of generations back. We bear more than a passing resemblance. What about you?"

"A sister of my great grandmother who was painted as a child. I looked very like her when I was really young, but the likeness diluted with age."

"What an interesting topic of study—family traits," said Rupert. "I wonder just how they are passed on and the reason things skip generations."

"Perhaps far in the future scientists will discover how to unlock those mysteries."

"Never." He swerved sharply around a corner causing Dodo to clutch her hat and break into peals of laughter.

"I never get tired of that," he said.

She squeezed his hand on the gear lever. "Now, let's talk about our other suspects. Is Hugh still under suspicion with the police?"

"I talked to Rosamund yesterday," he told her.

"What did she say?"

"She said the heat is off a little as the police are looking into other people with links to the gambling ring and polo. However, because Hugh had means, motive, and opportunity he is still a person of interest. But he has an alibi for the murder of the groom. He and Rosamund were together at a park."

"What is Rosamund's position on all of it?"

"She does not believe Hugh murdered Rafe, but she did tell me she is breaking off the engagement."

136

"Why? They seem so happy." This was a development Dodo had not foreseen.

"She is still very fond of him but she blames his temper. It seems to be getting worse. She's fearful of a future where he is unkind to their children. She doesn't want that."

"How is Hugh taking it?" she asked.

"He's a wreck. Rosamund is the love of his life, and he says it won't be worth living if she won't have him."

They drove in silence for several moments under another canopy of trees that caused the sun to sprinkle its rays on the car. Was there anywhere more marvelous than the English countryside when the sun was out?

"How about Jasper? He really needed your team to win to clear his debts. It's not much of a stretch to believe that he killed Rafe out of vengeance and desperation for hitting the winning shot?"

"It's possible I suppose, but I think he's more nervous about being roughed up for what he owes. And disappointing his family," said Rupert. "However, I think he'll try to make good on his threat to run away to South America, but I doubt he'll succeed because the police must be watching him since we filled them in on his involvement."

Dodo thought it was high time for a recap of evidence.

She referred to her notebook.

"There are so many facets to this case that it feels like a fast-growing tropical plant or a huge octopus," she said as the countryside whizzed by and various cows chewed the cud—their large, friendly faces hanging over wire fences. "We have several pieces of hard evidence. First, a pin from St. Helga's college. However, at this point, we don't know anyone that attended there."

"It's not that far from here. Do you want to swing by and ask about their alumni?" asked Rupert.

"Could we? If nothing comes of it, at least we'll know we tried."

Rupert looked at his watch. "We can be there in about forty minutes."

"Smashing." She looked at her notebook again. "Second, a matchbook with a distinctive emblem that neither the police nor we can trace."

"I've been thinking about that," said Rupert. "The SJP was approached by a company specializing in custom knickknacks for businesses. One of the items in their catalogue was personalized match books. I wasn't really interested since the whole point is to keep the underground jazz parties on the q.t. but I wonder if the one they found at the scene of Rafe's death could be a custom order created for an event or a private club?"

"Rupert you are a genius! Now that you say that, I remember at one of the weddings I attended with David there were bottles of champagne with the bride's family crest on the label. Perhaps that's it. How can we go about finding that out? Do you still have the details of the company?"

"Somewhere." He shifted down as they swung around another corner onto a narrow lane.

"I feel so much better when we have concrete leads to chase," she said. "And lastly, the maroon and white diamond scarf used to strangle the groom, Eddie Turnbull. His death ties the pin he found, directly to Rafe's murder."

"I keep thinking about that little fatherless girl and the surgery for her foot," said Rupert as they bumped across a ford. "I think I would like to make an anonymous donation."

Dodo turned her head sharply. "I agree one hundred percent. Let's do it! We can't bring her father back, but we *can* pay for the surgery her father died for." Dodo hadn't been sure she could love Rupert any more than she already did, but he had somehow managed it. She kissed his cheek as they plunged into an avenue of trees that blocked out the sun entirely.

"Alright, back to the scarf," Dodo said "We have seen Hugh with one, but it was not personally made for him and they are widely available. Add to that it was left at the restaurant, available to anyone to snatch. Is there time to stop by the restaurant as well?"

"I think we should go to St. Helga's first because I'm pretty sure their offices will close around five o'clock, but the restaurant should be open much later."

"Excellent."

St. Helga's College for Women was a former monastery. A lush green quad, surrounded by arched cloisters all funneled to a small, intimate chapel. The whole edifice was created from local stone, skillfully handcrafted by artisan masons from centuries before. Moss clung to the sides of the stone arches, much as the intellect of the students grasped the concepts of the classics and sciences. Though set in the heart of a bustling town, once inside its walls, the college gave the impression of being far out in the country.

Rupert's presence caused quite a stir among the female students walking along the cloisters in groups. After asking a group of young women to direct them to the office, Dodo and Rupert entered a spade-shaped black door, into an office bustling with activity.

Several older women were typing, one was sorting the post, and another answered the telephone. A thin, academic type with a tidy bun and wire rimmed spectacles looked down her nose at them from behind a battered counter. "Incoming student?" she asked Dodo.

"Oh, no!" said Dodo, her lip curling. "I've had all the schooling I care to."

The woman's smile froze.

"Not that I don't admire those who crave more," Dodo clarified. "I have nothing but respect for institutions such as this that improve the lot of women."

The fractured smile began to thaw.

"In fact, a relative of mine is a proud alumna of this revered college. Morgana Bloomfield."

"Miss Bloomfield?" said the clerk, all hostility melting clean away. "One of our most supportive alumnae. She raises funds for the college every year."

Dodo seized the opportunity being handed to her on a platter. "Indeed, that is why I'm here. My cousin wants me to compile a list of recent graduates to solicit for donations."

A look of confusion creased the woman's face. "But we have just had the annual fundraiser, not three weeks ago."

Drat! Think girl, think.

"As you know, Morgana is not one to let the grass grow under her feet and is eager to try a new method of fundraising for next year. She tasked me, Lady Dorothea Dorchester, with compiling the list." When the clerk showed a degree of hesitation, Dodo doubled down. "I live much closer to the college than Morgana, and she is currently on a European cruise."

One owlish eye squished into wrinkles. "I suppose it wouldn't hurt, then." The clerk tapped the counter with a hand. "If you will wait one moment, I'll search out the correct volumes."

"Thought you'd met your match there," whispered Rupert with a wicked grin, leaning on the battered wooden counter looking good enough to eat.

"Me too! It was dumb luck really and I was praying all the time that Morgana did not live right next to the college."

A couple of students came in to get their mail from the porter. As they waited, one got out a cigarette and her companion pulled out a matchbook to light it for her.

Dodo's heart stopped and she grabbed Rupert's arm.

The cover bore the very same emblem as the one found at the scene of Rafe's murder.

"I say," she said approaching the girls. "That is a captivating design. May I ask where you got those matches."

Both girls stared at her, before the one with long, blonde hair said, "There was a fundraising event here a few weeks ago. *Old Girls* or something like that. Anyway, there were some matchbooks left over so they brought them to the halls of residence for us to use."

"Oh," said Dodo, unable to take her eyes off the design. "I don't suppose you have any more? I've run out."

The students softened and the other girl, with short, cropped, dark hair, reached into her blazer pocket. "I have loads. You're welcome to one."

Dodo took the matchbook, eyes gleaming in triumph, as the girls left and returned to Rupert's side.

"Now we just have to find out what connection this women's college has to Rafe."

"Here are the first two volumes." The clerk handed them a couple of large leather tomes. "We close in an hour so be sure to get them back to me by then. There are benches in the cloisters you can use."

Dodo's heart began to beat faster. They were getting close.

They found a bench and looked at the spines. One was for years from the last century and the other, for all those who had attended since 1910.

"I think we should start with this one," she said holding up the newer edition.

Rather than print, each student's name was recorded in the finest copperplate handwriting. Dodo began dragging her finger down the vellum page.

"What are we looking for?" Rupert asked.

She pressed her lips together. "Not sure, but I'll know when we find it."

Page after page yielded no results.

"It's five minutes to five," said Rupert. Dodo was only three quarters of the way through.

"We might have to come back," said Dodo, keeping her eyes trained on the pages. "Perhaps you should scan the older version.

A clock began to chime the hour and Dodo's finger ran faster and faster down the columns as the cloisters filled with undergraduates spilling out of classes.

The efficient clerk from the office stepped out into the passage. "If you don't mind I need to take them back now. You're welcome to return another time."

One last page.

Dodo held up a finger to indicate that she was almost done. The woman tapped her toe, arms akimbo.

141

The top of the page said 1921.
Halfway down Dodo struck gold.
"Huzzah!"

Chapter 21

Dodo chattered through several theories the whole way to the restaurant they had been to with Hugh and Rosamund, bouncing her ideas off Rupert. By the time they reached the eatery, a solid hypothesis was evolving.

It was dinnertime and the restaurant was hopping. The maître d' looked up expectantly.

"Do you have a reservation?"

"Uh, no. We were wondering if we could ask you a few questions."

Another couple entered the establishment and the waiter looked past Dodo and Rupert, brows raised.

"I'm sorry, I'm rather busy. You'll have to wait." He indicated with his arm that they should stand to the side and checked in the couple as two more couples entered. Perhaps this was not such a good idea.

A group of four entered talking and gossiping, pushing Dodo and Rupert to the edges of the waiting area.

When the frazzled worker had finally seated all the customers, Dodo jumped up before a couple who were pulling at the door entered.

"Can I make a reservation for two?" Her stomach was growling, and the constant flow of people was a good indication that they would have to wait forever to speak to anyone.

The maître d' made a great show of pulling down his lip and looking through the reservation book.

"You are in luck. We have a table for two at eight." He raised a squashed smile.

Dodo glanced at her gold watch. *Twenty minutes.* "We'll take it."

She gave her name and returned to Rupert's side as a group of eight entered.

"Popular place," said Rupert with a smile that teetered on the edge of a laugh.

"That's why I just made a reservation," she explained. "Looks like it's the only way we'll get to talk to anyone tonight."

"Not a bad idea," he said, rubbing his hands together. "I'm actually starving."

Couple after couple poured through the door and the maître d's composure ebbed.

"Lady Dorothea," he finally called, brushing a hand across his flushed forehead. Two more couples entered. She and Rupert followed him through the tables until he stopped by the kitchen doors.

Dodo cocked a brow.

"This is all we have," responded the fellow, a challenge in his expression.

"Very well." Dodo picked up the menu, remembering how good their coquilles St Jacques had been.

"Good evening. My name is François, and I shall be your waiter tonight."

Biting back a smile, she looked up at the familiar voice. Rupert smothered a laugh. The bemused waiter cocked his head. "I remember you." His accent had slipped. "You were in here a few weeks ago when that chap stormed out."

"This really is serendipitous," declared Dodo. "Our friends left a scarf that night, and we forgot to take it home for them. I don't suppose you know what happened to it?"

"I know exactly where it went." He pulled on his black waistcoat. "I put it in the lost property. When I came in the next evening it was gone."

Dodo deflated. Another dead end. She grasped at one last straw. "Was it retrieved during the lunch shift?"

"Yes, my friend, Roberto"—he flicked a hand in the direction of another waiter—"he worked days that week and he told me that someone came in to get it."

"Do you think he would talk to us?" she asked.

"I can ask but as you can see, we're extremely busy tonight. Perhaps he will have time later."

Dodo and Rupert ordered their starters with a promise that François would ask Roberto to stop by their table later.

After enjoying their meal, they were getting ready to order dessert when Roberto approached them.

"I understand you are interested in knowing what happened to the red and white scarf," he said, hand slightly forward.

Rupert opened his wallet and discreetly passed him some money.

"A woman came in to reclaim it," the waiter explained.

Dodo described someone to him.

He nodded. "Yes. Exactly."

"Thank you, Roberto. You have been most helpful."

Dodo had taken the information she had uncovered at the college and restaurant to David and her mother. Lady Guinevere was of no help this time but within a few hours, David had come back with some very valuable insights.

"This one is complicated, isn't it, darling?" murmured David.

"Aren't they all," she lamented. "But I'm nearly there now."

"Be careful, Dodo."

She was building a thesis and all the pieces were finally coming together. Scotland Yard had not taken over the murder case from Inspector Bradford yet, but he was expecting them any day. When she shared what she had discovered with the inspector, he was more than happy to check on some of the loose ends. Solving this case before the *Sweeney* swooped in would be an impressive feather in his cap.

Polo was on hold, as were most other sports, until the web of deceit and loss of public trust had been resolved. Dodo had suggested to Rupert that they gather with his teammates on the night they should have played their second game of the season, positioned as a kind of memorial to Rafe. Lindley had agreed to host the meeting at the snazzy London flat and Rupert had catered the event through his contacts at the Savoy. Dodo had brought Lizzie and Ernie in to help serve.

145

Although Hugh and Rosamund had officially split up and were seated on opposite sides of the table, glowering at each other, the meal went well, with everyone but Rafe in attendance. The pre-dinner cocktails and wine helped promote a relaxed atmosphere. Rupert, Hugh, and Jasper shared funny stories about Rafe from their polo games and tales from childhood, as they ate.

As everyone pushed their dessert plates away and Ernie brought in the cheese, Lindley, as pre-arranged with Dodo, asked, "Does anyone know where the police are in their investigation?"

"Dodo has been working in tandem with them a bit," said Rupert. "She knows some of it, don't you, darling?"

"Tell us what you know," encouraged Lindley, as the casual atmosphere in the room tensed.

Dodo shrugged. "Do you really want to hear it? Isn't everyone sick of the thing?"

"No," said Lindley. "It seems only fitting at a memorial for Rafe, sitting in *his* apartment, that we know what happened."

"Well, if you insist," she said, running a nail across the white cloth. "First, I must tell you that there were a lot of red herrings in our path and few pieces of actual evidence. The first was something the inspector found the night of the murder, in the barn. He showed us a distinctive matchbook which neither of us recognized. It was the only strange thing that had been found at the scene. But frankly, it could have been dropped there at any time. Little did we know how important it would prove to be."

The room had become so quiet, a pin dropping would have sounded like cymbals crashing. She took a sip of wine to wet her whistle.

"Then when the gambling story broke, it seemed obvious to conclude that Rafe was involved, and on that strength, the case was about to be turned over to Scotland Yard. But for a recent breakthrough, it would have."

Someone coughed breaking the tension slightly.

"When the murder was first discovered, it seemed impossible that someone as affable and friendly as Rafe could have any enemies at all. But whoever had killed him had been exceptionally angry.

146

"For a long time, it appeared that Rafe was without the kind of vices that might lead to such a violent death, but as I said, the story of the sport's gambling hit the front pages and we all turned our sights in that direction."

Ordinary sounds drifted in from an open window, and Dodo thought how ironic it was that the life of someone in the room would be anything but normal by the time she was finished with her recitation.

"It was clear that Rafe needed money, and that the Alleyn estate was in bad shape," she continued. "Had Rafe started gambling with the organized ring in a desperate attempt to fill the family coffers?

"As the sports fixing house of cards began to collapse, more members of the polo team were implicated. At one point it seemed that no one was untouched. Jasper admitted to losing a great deal of money on that first game and our suspicions inclined to him."

Jasper tensed, looking like he was going to protest. She raised a hand.

"But Jasper did not know of any involvement by Rafe. How could that be if he too were embroiled in the conspiracy?

Relaxing back against his chair as if the danger for him was past, he reached for Juliette's hand.

"In fact, we learned that Jasper had bet *against* the team winning," Dodo continued. "But Rafe had made sure they won by hitting the ball through the goal, right before the whistle blew. If Rafe was in on the wager, he certainly would not have hit that winning goal. This was confusing to say the least.

"Additionally, the medical examiner had told us the murder was unlikely to have been committed by a woman and on the strength of that opinion I continued to direct my inquiries at all the men who had been there that fateful day."

Rosamund took out a cigarette case but left it sitting on the table.

Dodo stood and moved to the window. "His cousin the captain, became the earl due to Rafe's death, but it was soon apparent that the estate wasn't worth the paper the deed was printed on. This was hardly unknown to the captain since he had spent much time at

Farrow's End. Plus, he was now responsible for the fragile dowager's well-being."

Lizzie and Ernie entered the dining room and stood by the doors.

"Jasper had admitted to being angry about the outcome of the game, but we learned that his involvement was with Max Fortnon, a member of the opposing team, and someone to whom he now owed a great deal of money. Killing Rafe would not help Jasper pay his debts. He seemed an unlikely suspect at that point."

Juliette smiled with her eyes and squeezed Jasper's hand.

Crossing her ankles, Dodo perched on the window ledge. "The police had focused their attention on Hugh from the beginning. He had an uncontrollable temper and he certainly knew his way around the stables and a mallet. Also, Hugh admitted to going back to the changing rooms but claimed to leave Rafe alive and well, asserting that he had heard Rafe in an urgent conversation with someone. Unfortunately for him, no one could corroborate this. At least at the time of his arrest. And Hugh was furious when he discovered that Rafe and Rosamund had once been sweethearts and that they had kept it a secret from him. It looked like an open and shut case to the police.

"Meanwhile, my own investigations were opening up the secrets of the other actors in the drama. Max Fortnon was shown to be a nasty piece of work. He had started his nefarious activities as a boy, and they had only hardened as an adult. It was also uncovered that he was a major player in the sports fixing scheme. I could easily see him killing Rafe out of anger for winning the game.

"But then the groom was killed. Again, the police were convinced that the crime could not have been carried out by a woman. How could a female carry the dead weight of a man and place him in a barrel? The finger pointed straight back to Max. If the groom had witnessed the murder and blackmailed Max Fortnon, it was not a stretch to imagine him executing the groom to keep him quiet."

Dodo had calculated that suspicion directed at Max would result in a shift in the atmosphere of the smoky room. Her speculation paid off. Tense shoulders dropped, tight eyes softened. It was the perfect condition to hurl her darts at the unsuspecting crowd.

"But the groom had an alibi for the murder of Rafe. How could he have witnessed the fatal beating if he was not even at the club during the window of time the attack was carried out?

"Rupert and I took a trip to visit the grieving widow who confirmed her husband's alibi but in an interesting twist, revealed to us that Eddie had found something he believed the killer had dropped, several days after the murder while he was cleaning out the stables." Lizzie handed her the item and Dodo held it up. All but one person peered to get a better look.

"A tie pin with a horseshoe emblem engraved on it that Eddie soon connected to the murderer. His daughter needed expensive surgery, so he made the dangerous choice to exploit his finding—to his everlasting regret.

"Meanwhile, we discovered that Rafe had modernized this London flat. With what money? Certainly nothing declared as part of the estate. And worse…" She paused and looked at the grave expressions around the room. "…that he had been doping his horses."

"What?" cried Jasper, slapping the top of the table? "I can't believe it."

"It's true," confirmed Rupert. "A witness saw him administering the stuff to his horse that day, and I found a vial of hops stashed in the floor of this very apartment."

"So, you can see how this clouded the way," continued Dodo. "But it also proved that Rafe was not as 'clean' as we had all believed. Hot on the heels of that discovery, the inspector revealed the details of the scarf that had been used to strangle the groom."

"We had seen it before," added Rupert.

Hugh shifted in his chair.

"But it had been left in a public restaurant where anyone could have picked it up," Rupert disclosed.

"We now had three solid clues," Dodo resumed. "The pin with a horseshoe on it, a matchbook with a snake emblem and a colorful scarf known to belong to one of the team members. But I could not figure out how they were linked."

A slight noise made Dodo pause but everyone else in the room was riveted by her story.

"Quite by chance, I was doodling the omega, or upside-down horseshoe, insignia from the pin when someone recognized it, only they pointed out that I had it upside down. It was not a horseshoe. It was an inverted omega, a physics symbol used by St. Helga's Women's College as their emblem.

"We visited the college to check their roster and discovered that the very matchbook that had been found at the scene of the crime had been given out at a fundraiser a few weeks before. Now things were getting clearer. A quick trip to the restaurant to see who, if anyone, had picked up the scarf, and we were almost home free."

Glances bounced around the room like flies trapped in a jar.

"I now had the 'who', but I was stumped on the means because of what the doctor and the inspector had told me about the murders needing strength." Dodo stood, and pulling back the net curtains, looked out the window to the street beneath. "That is, until I considered the possibility of that person having an accomplice."

A murmur ran around the room.

"And I was still stumped on the 'why'."

A minor sound from beyond the doors was expertly covered by Ernie clearing his throat.

Dodo tipped her head in appreciation then carried on with her conclusions. "I shared my new theory with Inspector Bradford and we both began searching for a motive."

Leaving the cool air of the window, Dodo placed her hands on the back of Rupert's chair. "And one more thing bothered me. If two people claimed to have met before and only one was alive to tell about it, could you be sure you were getting the whole truth?"

She walked halfway around the table, all heads swiveling to follow her.

"Would it surprise you to know that Rafe *was* betting on the games?" Another ripple of murmurs. "Not with the nationwide ring. His operation was on a much smaller scale. But who was *his* bookie if not Max? Turns out it was someone he had known for a long time."

"Rosamund!" cried Hugh, pointing at her across the table. "I knew it! I knew you were lying about your relationship with him. I—"

"You're delusional. Sit down, you fool!" Rosamund snarled.

Rupert and Lindley stood and slowly moved toward the doors and all eyes at the table stared at the beautiful redhead.

"According to London gossip, one of the underground casinos is run by a woman. An educated lady who, even as a girl, showed signs of an exceptional talent for cards," disclosed Dodo. "She was almost thrown out of St. Helga's for taking so much money from her fellow students." Rosamund turned the silver cigarette case in her hands.

"Rosamund told me of her former relationship with Rafe, which I took at face value. But Rafe was no longer around to verify her account. She had emphasized how insignificant their relationship had been when she was young and downplayed their reunion.

"However, Rafe must have known about her bent for gambling and when they met again through Hugh, I imagine Rafe mentioned his money woes to Rosamund who was more than happy to inform him of a lucrative way to make a lot of cash. So began a mutually beneficial arrangement. Rafe had bet on you all to *win* the game, hence his wild delight when he scored. It was the answer to all of his financial problems. But success makes people greedy and I'm guessing he wanted more of the pie." Dodo spun on the spot to face the accused. "Am I right, Rosamund?"

Rosamund had finally pulled out a cigarette and was lighting it with a snake matchbook from St. Helga's. She clapped slowly. "Bravo!" She took a long drag, letting a curl of smoke wind its way up to the chandelier, eyeing the men at the dining room doors. "Rafe was acting conspicuously, splashing his money around on this place and I was concerned he would end up making a mistake by telling the wrong person where his money came from. I couldn't have that. It would compromise my whole operation. I demanded he tone things down, but he told me not to worry."

151

Hugh moved his chair ever so slightly, beads of sweat shining on his upper lip.

"However," Rosamund continued, "an uncle of mine is friends with the police commissioner—he has been an extremely useful idiot. Through him I learned that the police were onto a large gambling endeavor. At first, I worried it was mine. I thought Rafe had already been indiscreet." She tapped the ash from her cigarette on her plate and crossed her arms.

"I came to the first game and saw Rafe recklessly revel in his win and knew he had to be stopped. I borrowed a black cape I saw on a hook, ran into the changing rooms and begged Rafe to be sensible. He told me I was worrying about nothing. That he wasn't stupid. But I knew him. I knew he had a hard time keeping a secret and he wasn't taking the situation seriously." She glared around the room daring anyone to contradict her. "I had an empire to protect!

"There wasn't much time to plan. I had to act fast. I slipped back to the barn while Hugh was chatting, waited for Rafe to come and spoil his horse as he always did, and put an end to the problem." She sighed. "I thought I had been so careful. When I got a message from the groom, I was knocked for six. I arranged to meet him at the stables and brought Hugh along but left him in the club bar. I took his scarf, that I had retrieved from the restaurant, as insurance. He was already the main suspect so I thought it would help to throw fuel on the fire. I was tired of him. He had ruined things between us with that temper of his."

Hugh's face was turning every shade of white. He was looking at Rosamund as though she were a stranger, with eyes scorched by betrayal.

"The stupid groom underestimated me. He didn't even see me coming, which made killing him easy." Rosamund took another drag on the cigarette. "I dragged him behind some hay but knew that wasn't a suitable long-term plan. So, I ran back to get Hugh. I told him it was a terrible accident and I needed his help to hide the body. He was so scared he didn't even notice his scarf was there." She stubbed out the cigarette. "I suppose it's all over now."

At a signal from Dodo, Rupert opened the door to the dining area and the inspector, and a crowd of police officers, entered. If Rosamund had entertained the idea of running, their entrance put paid to the notion.

Everyone else at the table stared at Rosamund in horror.

"Rosamund Ainsworth, I am arresting you for the murders of Raphael Alleyn and Edward Turnbull."

In the end, Rosamund was surprisingly cavalier, and Dodo wondered if she had put a drug in her own drink while Dodo was laying out the crime. Hugh, on the other hand, was frantic and kept thrashing his arms to avoid the handcuffs until a couple of police officers got rough and pinned his hands behind his back.

"Steady on!" he cried as they dragged him out. "I didn't kill anyone!"

Ernie closed the doors to the dining room as if to signal the end of the drama.

"That was amazing," said Poppy. "I half thought you were going to accuse me!"

"Fortunately, you and the captain were the only ones we didn't find any dirt on," Dodo responded. "Though we did wonder about the captain for a while."

Lindley sidled over and placed an arm around Poppy's shoulders and Dodo's brows rose.

Poppy ducked her head. "I called to see how things were going after all that kerfuffle with the photos in the newspaper," she explained.

"She came over and we hit it off," Lindley said. "We were going to keep it confidential a little longer but after that charade, I think it's time to be open. I feel so much better having someone to talk to and lean on." He bent his head down to Poppy's. "I just cannot believe it. Rosamund seemed so agreeable. How can she be a double murderer?"

"Murderers do not wear their crimes on their faces. It would make policing a whole lot easier if they did!" declared Dodo.

"Will those photos that were published affect anything?" Rupert asked.

"My solicitor thinks not, and Russell seems to be an honorable man. I don't think he will tell. Without his testimony they don't have a leg to stand on."

They all stood mute as the clanging of the sirens split the air as the police cars took Rosamund and Hugh away.

Chapter 22

H aving survived the legal challenge to the earldom, Lindley had successfully pulled off a village fair at the estate. After selling off a small portion of land for new houses on the far east side, he and his accountant concluded that opening the estate to the public for a set period of time each year was the answer to his financial woes. The fair was to introduce the villagers to the estate as well as raise funds and Lindley hoped to make it an annual event.

Dodo and Rupert, along with Lizzie and Ernie, had come to support the new earl's latest venture. A hairy coconut sat on the table between them, evidence of Ernie's prowess with a ball.

There were horse rides for children, various stalls encouraging people to try their luck, cream teas, and friendly races along the lines of egg and spoon.

The weather had been more than accommodating and Dodo was parched.

"Thanks for coming," said Lindley, Poppy Drinkwater on his arm looking fabulous in cream chiffon. "Looks like this is going to be a profitable venture and the sale of the land has provided the funds for the roof."

"I am so glad to hear it, Lindley," said Dodo. "And the dowager is looking so much better." Dodo looked toward Rafe's mother who was leading young children around a temporary paddock on a pony.

Lindley followed Dodo's gaze. "I involved her in the planning, and it was amazing to see her perk up. We turned to each other in our grief and she has become a surrogate mother for me."

"What a happy outcome."

"I have kept all the details about Rafe's death from her, and she never reads the paper so it has been easy to fashion the narrative into something less sordid. Hopefully, she will die believing her son to be a paragon of virtue. She certainly won't hear otherwise from me. Now, if you will excuse us, I have others I need to see."

"Of course," said Dodo.

"Did you read the announcement that Lady Florence Tingey is engaged?" said Poppy as they turned to leave.

"Yes, I saw it in the Times," she replied.

"What was that about?" asked Lizzie, as Ernie wiped cream from her mouth with a spotless handkerchief.

"A cautionary tale," said Dodo and told Lizzie about Lady Florence's sad history that was not likely to have a happy ending.

"Her true love was your friend?" Lizzie asked Rupert.

"It appears so. Now that he's gone and there is no chance of a reconciliation, I suppose she doesn't care. But she will have a sorry life with that brute."

"What do you think Jasper and Juliette's chances for happiness are?" Dodo asked Rupert.

"I hear that one does not need much to live on in South America but being a fugitive, unable to return to one's country of birth, may take its toll. One needs more to live on than love."

"And I thought you were a hopeless romantic," said Dodo, chucking Rupert's chin.

"I am where you are concerned," he chuckled.

"What will you do about polo?" asked Ernie. "Your whole team has vanished."

Rupert leaned back, legs stretched out, crossed at the ankles. "That, my man, is the question. This whole season has been written off, of course, but do I make the effort to solicit a brand new team or do I lay my mallet down to rest?"

"Oh, that would be a pity, sir, if you don't mind me saying so," said Ernie. "It is a noble sport and now that it has been purged in the crucible, so to speak, I think it will rise stronger from the ashes."

"Perhaps you could ask the Prince of Wales if he needs a player," said Dodo with a glint in her eye.

"Very funny. But there are a lot of teams in shambles as the tentacles of the gambling operation have been cut off by the police. Perhaps I will try and scrape together a new team."

"That would be very wise, sir," said Ernie.

Dodo kicked Rupert under the table.

"And what about you, Ernie?" said Rupert, rubbing his shin. "What new risks are you taking?"

Ernie's face fell. "I think I may have to train for a new career, sir. The war had more of an effect on society than I had appreciated. As the old guard dies off, the newer members of high society are doing away with valets and becoming independent. I can see the writing on the wall and the money I make as a waiter is not enough to support my parents. I should hate for my father to have to go back to work at his age. I thought I might go and train as a journalist or an accountant."

"That would be a shame," said Rupert. "But I see the dilemma. I simply don't have the room at my little mews house for any staff." He cleared his throat. "But did I mention I have bought a new property in town?"

"The town house lost by Jasper in his gambling?" Dodo asked, playing her part with an eye on Lizzie who was gazing off into the distance.

"The very one," said Rupert. "It had become part of a police auction since it was a profit gained from an illegal enterprise, and I won it. Got it for a song, really. It is a valuable investment that will pay great dividends. There is just one problem."

"And what is that?" asked Dodo innocently.

"I need someone to run it for me." Rupert stared straight at Ernie.

Sounds came out of Ernie's mouth that may have been words, but Dodo couldn't be sure. Lizzie turned her head sharply.

Rupert spread his fingers out on the table. "I am asking you to be my valet-butler and to run my new townhome. Are you interested in the job?"

"You want me to be your wingman?" Ernie finally managed, eyes wide as plates.

"Couldn't have put it better myself. Are you in?" A slick smile spread over his beloved features.

"A-a-are you kidding, sir? I can start today if you like."

"You haven't even asked the terms," said Rupert with a twinkle.

Ernie shook his head. "It is what I love, sir. And it will be more than I make as a waiter. I'm more grateful than you will ever know."

157

"Well, that's not enough for me," said Rupert sliding a folded piece of paper toward the astonished valet. "I like things to be written out in black and white."

Ernie opened the paper and a sound like a sob tried to escape his throat. With shining eyes, he held out his hand. "That is very generous, sir. I accept."

Rupert shook his hand. "Nonsense! You are a man of great experience and tireless work ethic, and you will be required to do the work of several men. That salary only reflects what you are worth."

Ernie used the handkerchief to wipe his eyes and then slipped from his chair onto his knees.

Lizzie let out a small shriek.

"Elizabeth Prudence Perkins," Ernie began in a voice strangled with emotions. "Will you do me the honor of agreeing to be my wife?"

Tears rolled down Lizzie's creamy cheeks and she glanced at Dodo whose own eyes were stinging.

"Yes! Of course! Yes!" Lizzie leaned down and clasped Ernie to her as they sobbed together. Rupert reached for Dodo's hand.

"I have only been waiting to get a job so that I can give you the life you deserve," said Ernie, hauling himself back onto the chair. "I wasn't much of a catch as a waiter and didn't want you to feel shackled to me. But now…" He shone a smile of gratitude at Rupert. "It will have to be a long engagement so I can save up. My savings have all depleted since my last employer died."

"I don't care," said Lizzie through happy tears. "You are well worth the wait Ernest Scott!"

Dodo brushed a hand across her cheek and looked at Rupert through shimmering eyes as he winked back at her like a proud father.

How had she got so lucky?

"Perhaps it will be our turn soon," he whispered in her ear.

The End

Thanks for buying my book!

Ann Sutton

I hope you enjoyed book 9, *Murder Takes a Swing* and love Dodo as much as I do.

I am pleased to announce that I have created a new series, the Percy Pontefract Mysteries. Book 1, *Death at a Christmas Party: A 1920's Cozy Mystery,* is available now on Amazon.

https://amzn.to/3Qb4BhG

A merry Christmas party with old friends. A dead body in the kitchen. A reluctant heroine. Sounds like a recipe for a jolly festive murder mystery!

"It is 1928 and a group of old friends gather for their annual Christmas party. The food, drink and goodwill flow, and everyone has a rollicking good time.

When the call of nature forces the accident-prone Percy Pontefract up, in the middle of the night, she realizes she is in need of a little midnight snack and wanders into the kitchen. But she gets more than she bargained for when she trips over a dead body.

Ordered to remain in the house by the grumpy inspector sent to investigate the case, Percy stumbles upon facts about her friends that shake her to the core and cause her to suspect more than one of them of the dastardly deed.

Finally permitted to go home, Percy tells her trusty cook all the awful details. Rather than sympathize, the cook encourages her to do some investigating of her own. After all, who knows these people better than Percy? Reluctant at first, Percy begins poking into her friends' lives, discovering they all harbor dark secrets. However, none seem connected to the murder...at first glance.

Will Percy put herself and her children in danger before she can solve the case that has the police stumped?"

Interested in a **free** prequel to the Dodo Dorchester Mystery series?

Go to https://dl.bookfunnel.com/997vvive24 to download *Mystery at the Derby.*

Book 1 of the series, *Murder at Farrington Hall* is available on Amazon.

https://amzn.to/31WujyS

"Dodo is invited to a weekend party at Farrington Hall. She and her sister are plunged into sleuthing when a murder occurs. Can she solve the crime before Scotland Yard's finest?"

Book $\mathcal{2}$ of the series, *Murder is Fashionable* is available on Amazon.

https://amzn.to/2HBshwT

"Stylish Dodo Dorchester is a well-known patron of fashion. Hired by the famous Renee Dubois to support her line of French designs, she travels between Paris and London frequently. Arriving for the showing of the Spring 1923 collection, Dodo is thrust into her role as an amateur detective when one of the fashion models is murdered. Working under the radar of the French DCJP Inspector Roget, she follows clues to solve the crime. Will the murderer prove to be the man she has fallen for?"

Book *3* of the series, *Murder at the Races* is available on Amazon.

https://amzn.to/2QIdYKM

"It is royal race day at Ascot, 1923. Lady Dorothea Dorchester, Dodo, has been invited by her childhood friend, Charlie, to an exclusive party in a private box with the added incentive of meeting the King and Queen.

Charlie appears to be interested in something more than friendship when a murder interferes with his plans. The victim is one of the guests from the box and Dodo cannot resist poking around. When Chief Inspector Blood of Scotland Yard is assigned to the case, sparks fly between them again. The chief inspector and Dodo have worked together on a case before and he welcomes her assistance with the prickly upper-class suspects. But where does this leave poor Charlie?

Dodo eagerly works on solving the murder which may have its roots in the distant past. Can she find the killer before they strike again?"

Book *4* of the series, *Murder on the Moors* is available on Amazon.

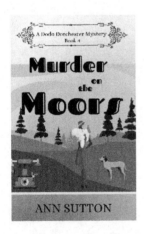

When you just want to run away and nurse your broken heart but murder comes knocking.

"Lady Dorothea Dorchester, Dodo, flees to her cousins' estate in Dartmoor in search of peace and relaxation after her devastating break-up with Charlie and the awkward attraction to Chief Inspector Blood that caused it.
Horrified to learn that the arch-nemesis from her schooldays, Veronica Shufflebottom, has been invited, Dodo prepares for disappointment. However, all that pales when one of the guests disappears after a ramble on the foggy moors. Presumed dead, Dodo attempts to contact the local police to report the disappearance only to find that someone has tampered with the ancient phone. The infamous moor fog is too thick for safe travel and the guests are therefore stranded.
Can Dodo solve the case without the help of the police before the fog lifts?"

Book 5 of the series, *Murder in Limehouse* is available on Amazon.

https://amzn.to/3pw2wzQ

Aristocratic star she may be, but when her new love's sister is implicated in a murder, Dodo Dorchester rolls up her designer sleeves and plunges into the slums of London.

Dodo is back from the moors of Devon and diving into fashion business for the House of Dubois with one of the most celebrated department stores in England, while she waits for a call from Rupert Danforth, her newest love interest.
Curiously, the buyer she met with at the store, is murdered that night in the slums of Limehouse. It is only of passing interest because Dodo has no real connection to the crime. Besides, pursuing the promising relationship that began in Devon is a much higher priority.

However, fate has a different plan. Rupert's sister, Beatrice, is arrested for the murder of the very woman Dodo conducted business with at the fashionable store. Now she must solve the crime to protect the man she is fast falling in love with.

Can she do it before Beatrice is sent to trial?

Book *6* of the series, *Murder on Christmas Eve,* is available on Amazon.

Dodo is invited to meet Rupert's family for Christmas. What could possibly go wrong?

Fresh off the trauma of her last case, Dodo is relieved when Rupert suggests spending Christmas with his family at Knightsbrooke Priory.
The week begins with such promise until Rupert's grandmother, Adelaide, dies in the middle of their Christmas Eve dinner. She is ninety-five years old and the whole family considers it an untimely natural death, but something seems off to Dodo who uses the moment of shock to take a quick inventory of the body. Certain clues bring her to draw the conclusion that Adelaide has been murdered, but this news is not taken well.
With multiple family skeletons set rattling in the closets, the festive week of celebrations goes rapidly downhill and Dodo fears that Rupert's family will not forgive her meddling. Can she solve the case and win back their approval?

Book *7* of the series, *Murder on the Med* is available on Amazon

https://amzn.to/3PooO99

An idyllic Greek holiday. A murdered ex-pat. Connect the victim to your tourist party, and you have a problem that only Dodo can solve.

Dodo's beau, Rupert, is to meet the Dorchesters for the first time on their annual Greek holiday. He arrives in Athens by train and her family accept him immediately. But rather than be able to enjoy private family time, an eclectic group of English tourists attach themselves to the Dorchesters, and insist on touring the Parthenon with them.

Later that night, a body is found in the very area they had visited and when Dodo realizes that it is the woman she saw earlier, near the hotel, staring at someone in their group, she cannot help but get involved. The over-worked and under-staffed local detective is more than happy for her assistance and between them they unveil all the tourists' dirty secrets.

With help from Rupert and Dodo, can the detective discover the murderer and earn himself a promotion?

Book *8* of the series, *Murder Spoils the Fair* is available on Amazon

https://amzn.to/42xldFn

A high profile national fair, a murdered model. Can Dodo solve the crime before it closes the fair?

The historic British Empire Fair of 1924 is set to be officially opened by the king at the new Wembley Stadium and Lady Dorothea Dorchester, Dodo, has an invitation.

The whole fair is an attempt to build morale after a devastating World War and the planning and preparation have been in the works for years. So much is riding on its success.

The biggest soap maker in England has been offered the opportunity to host a beauty exhibit and after a nationwide search for the ten most beautiful girls in Britain, they build an extravagant 'palace' that will feature live models representing famous women of history, including one who will represent today's modern woman. Dodo has succeeded in winning the bid to clothe Miss 1924 with fashions from the House of Dubois for whom she is a fashion ambassador.

But the fair has hardly begun when disaster strikes. One of the models is murdered. Can Dodo find the murderer before the bad PR closes the fair?

For more information about the series go to my website at www.annsuttonauthor.com and subscribe to my newsletter.

You can also follow me on Facebook at:
https://www.facebook.com/annsuttonauthor

About the Author

Agatha Christie plunged me into the fabulous world of reading when I was 10. I was never the same. I read every one of her books I could lay my hands on. Mysteries remain my favorite genre to this day - so it was only natural that I would eventually write my own.

Born and raised in England, writing fiction about my homeland keeps me connected.

After finishing my degree in French and Education and raising my family, writing has become a favorite hobby.

I hope that Dame Agatha would enjoy Dodo Dorchester at much as I do.

Acknowledgements

I would like to thank all those who have read my books, write reviews and provide suggestions as you continue to inspire.

I would also like to thank my critique partners, Mary Malcarne Thomas and Lisa McKendrick

So many critique groups are overly critical. I have found with you guys a happy medium of encouragement, cheerleading and constructive suggestions. Thank you.

My proof-reader – Tami Stewart

The mothers of a large and growing families who read like the wind with an eagle eye. Thank you for finding little errors that have been missed.

My editor – Jolene Perry of Waypoint Author Academy

Sending my work to editors is the most terrifying part of the process for me but Jolene offers correction and constructive criticism without crushing my fragile ego.

My cheerleader, marketer and IT guy – Todd Matern

A lot of the time during the marketing side of being an author I am running around with my hair on fire. Todd is the yin to my yang. He calms me down and takes over when I am yelling at the computer.

My beta readers – Francesca Matern, Stina Van Cott,

Your reactions to my characters and plot are invaluable.

The Writing Gals for their FB author community and their YouTube tutorials

These ladies give so much of their time to teaching their Indie author followers how to succeed in this brave new publishing world. Thank you.

Printed in Great Britain
by Amazon

22456174R00106